Joaquin and his wife came to California, young and in love. They dreamed of a home in the new land, and wealth in the gold fields—until Roberts and his gang found their claim. In one hour, their peaceful life became a trail of vengeance, as Joaquin led others of his countrymen in a futile endeavour to resist the terrible *Americanos* as he became a national hero of the Hispanic people in North America.

TRAIL OF VENGEANCE

TRAIL OF
VENGEANCE

Louis Kretschman

A BERKLEY MEDALLION BOOK
published by
BERKLEY PUBLISHING CORPORATION

to Lois...
joyously, we shared the heartache

Lester Lewis Associates, Inc.
156 East 52nd Street
New York, N.Y. 10022

SBN 425-03461-5

*BERKLEY MEDALLION BOOKS are published by
Berkley Publishing Corporation
200 Madison Avenue
New York, N.Y. 10016*

BERKLEY MEDALLION BOOK ® TM 757,375

Printed in the United States of America

Berkley Medallion Edition, AUGUST, 1977

Prologue

A crowd was becoming a mob at the corner of Kearny and Commercial Streets.

In front of an Army field tent which was the headquarters of the San Francisco Society of Regulators (more generally known as the Hounds), a roughly dressed, bearded miner stood on a plank placed across two shipping crates, beating a large drum. The throbbing beat continued, and the men gathered there began to push and jostle each other as the crowd swelled.

Down the sloping hillside covered with a disorderly array of ragged tents, some made of canvas and others made of flour bags and calico stretched on wooden frames, hurried more men. From the few log-and-board shanties on Kearny Street, from two frame saloons, one on each corner of Commercial Street, others came to join the crowd. Laughing and boisterous, they stumbled and supported each other in the deep ruts of the wheel-tracked earthen street. Shoving good-naturedly, they crowded toward the tent of the Regulators which had the name TAMMANY HALL emblazoned in large letters on a banner above the tent's entrance.

Another man stepped onto the plank platform beside

the drummer. He was dressed in full regimental uniform and the crowd greeted him with crude familiarity.

"Hey, Sam!" the men yelled. "Lookie, there's the Capt'n all dressed up for parade! Ho, Capt'n Roberts!" they called out.

Clean-shaven and resplendent in his uniform, Samuel Roberts waved and shouted back, calling many of the raggedly dressed, unshaven men by name. Roberts had come to San Francisco in March of 1847, a member of Company E, of Colonel Jonathan D. Stevenson's regiment of volunteers, recruited in New York City to fight in the war with Mexico. The troops had been discharged from the Army by October, 1848, whereupon Roberts had given himself the rank of lieutenant and organized the Society of Regulators. Now he called for order and tried to be heard over the beating of the drum.

The crowd shouted back and the miner with the drum continued to beat it as loud as he could.

Farther down Commercial Street, two swarthy-skinned men wearing large straw hats, Mexicans, who had been in the gold fields long enough to know of the Regulators, saw the crowd in front of Tammany Hall and quickly slipped in beside a building and disappeared.

It was Sunday, July 15, 1849.

Roberts suddenly took command of the situation by knocking the drummer off the platform. Then, as the crowd exploded with raucous laughter, he drew a pistol and fired two shots into the ground. The meeting had been called to order.

Now he addressed the silent and attentive audience. "Gentlemen, you all know the Society of Regulators

2

stands for law and order.'' He paused to let the crowd voice agreement. ''And to see that justice is done.'' Another pause while the men shouted their approval. ''And to insure that—as my good friend and commander, General Persifor F. Smith, United States Army, put it—that 'only native Americans are entitled to share the riches of this great state of California.' ''

The crowd yelled vigorous affirmation and Sam Roberts paused, appraising the individual men. All emigrants, they were a new breed in what had been Alta California, in Mexico. Rough, hard-working, boisterous men, dressed in flannel shirts and patched woolen pants stuffed into knee-high boots; tough, strong men because only the strongest had survived the unbelievable hardships of the trip to the gold fields in '49. On the other side of Commercial Street, a few businessmen, an aproned storekeeper, two gamblers, and some fashionably dressed whores were in the crowd but not part of it.

Roberts silenced the crowd as two Regulators, in partial Army uniforms, dragged a short, swarthy man wearing a *serape*, and holding a straw *sombrero* in his hands, onto the platform.

A storekeeper stepped up on the other side of Roberts, took off his apron, and doffed his hat to the restless crowd.

''Gentlemen,'' Roberts addressed the audience, ''a foul injustice has been perpetrated against an American citizen by this *Chileno*.''

The man in the *serape* understood only a few of the English words, but he interpreted the ominous murmur of the crowd and began to speak rapidly in a flow of

3

musical Spanish, protesting whatever the accusation might be.

"What's he say?" called someone in the crowd. "Make him speak English!"

Roberts raised both hands for silence and turned to the storekeeper. "George Frank, tell them your grievance. We want to reach a fair decision here."

"I grubstaked 'im, that's what I did," said the storekeeper. "Shoulda known better than to do business with a dirty *Chileno*, but he comes to me last October with a tale about a motherlode and I give him what he asks for." He dug in his pocket and produced a bill of sale which he handed to Roberts. "There's the list of stuff I gave him and there's his name, Pedro Cueta, and there's his mark to show he got it."

Sam Roberts examined the paper. He turned to the South American. "Are you Pedro Cueta?"

"Sí, sí," said the *Chileno*.

Roberts extended the bill of sale. "That your mark?"

"Sí."

Roberts turned to George Frank. "Won't he pay you?"

"No, he paid me the bill, all right," said the storekeeper indignantly. "But he come back with two mules loaded with gold and I'm claiming half his strike."

The crowd began to stir, the men talking among themselves and shouting up to the platform. Pedro Cueta protested in rapid Spanish. Sam Roberts raised his hands for silence.

"Is that a fair claim?" he asked the crowd.

The men shouted their approval of the storekeeper's

4

claim and their overwhelming disapproval of all *Chilenos*.

Roberts turned to the storekeeper. "George Frank, you have a just claim. Take one of those mules and the gold."

"That's it! I can't!" explained George Frank. "The dirty greaser and some of his friends have hid the gold, or carried it out of town."

The crowd reacted violently. Those at the rear pushed forward. Those near the platform reached for the already condemned *Chileno*. Pedro Cueta shrank back, behind Captain Roberts, as he poured forth a stream of Spanish, the words all running together in a frantic plea for justice.

Roberts pushed him away and smoothed his regimental dress uniform where greaser hands had touched it. He addressed the crowd of shouting, excited miners.

"Gentlemen! Gentlemen! You heard the testimony. What's your verdict?"

"String him up! Hang him!"

Sam Roberts tried to restore order, but the crowd would not be silenced. They wanted justice. They wanted blood.

"Listen to me!" Roberts shouted, but they wouldn't listen. They hauled Pedro Cueta from the platform and were preparing to hang him when Roberts fired his pistol again.

"Listen to me!" Roberts repeated. "It's been a fair trial and I say that George Frank has a just claim."

The men yelled agreement and Roberts continued. "But I say that gold is still here . . . hidden somewhere . . . in the Mexican quarter." The crowd stilled, sensing something more. "And I say let's go there and find it—even if we have to rip apart every shack and shanty in the quarter!"

In one roaring voice the crowd voted agreement and, in that moment, it became a mob set upon vengeance and plunder. Pedro Cueta was dragged to one of the saloons at the corner of Commercial Street and hanged from a rafter supporting a second-floor balcony. It took only minutes for the men to arm themselves with guns, knives, pickaxes, clubs and shovels, and follow the dauntless Captain Roberts to the Mexican quarter.

The authors of *The Annals of San Francisco*, who saw the malicious attack, wrote: "Without provocation, and in cold blood, they barbarously beat with sticks and stones and cuffed and kicked the unoffending foreigners. Not content with that, they repeatedly and wantonly fired among the injured people and, amid the shrieks of terrified women and the groans of wounded men, recklessly continued their terrible course wherever malice or thirst for plunder led them. . . ."

The nighttime streets of Clark's Point were as bright as daylight in front of each saloon and bordello. Piano music and plunking banjos could be heard through swinging doors. A group of eight carousing Regulators burst out of one saloon and paused for a moment, in loud conversation, before they moved on to the saloon next down the line. They filled the board sidewalk as they continued on their way.

In the darkness between the lighted saloons, a Chinaman stepped into the mud and ruts of the street to let them pass.

"Heathen Chinee!" one of the Regulators cried, alerting the group.

"They scubber their own daughters," another informed the group.

"And they eat rats and birdshit and rotten eggs!"

The group laughed and jostled each other, moving on, intent only on getting to the next saloon.

Hands in his sleeves, the Chinaman stood with eyes downcast, his face impassive. As the last of the Regulators passed, he softly quoted a line from Confucius, about the dignity of man.

"What's he say!" a Regulator yelled and the group turned and swarmed over the Chinaman. One held him by his queue while another cut out his tongue. Then, to release him, the first Regulator cut off his queue.

The Chinaman, making horrible gasping sounds, sputtering blood and spittle, held one hand to his mouth, the other to his cut queue, as he sank to his knees in the mud of the street.

Laughing and joking, the eight Regulators moved on.

Shrouded in the morning mists which always cloaked this bay area until the sun rose high enough to burn it off, a noisy mob of forty-niners was dragging a woman from a board shanty on Telegraph Hill, the vice-ridden red-light district of San Francisco.

The woman was Mexican, in her late twenties, voluptuous and full-bodied, with wavy dark hair that hung loose to her waist. She wore only a light, almost transparent, cambric smock which kept opening and she struggled as desperately to hide her body as she did against her tormentors as they dragged her to a nearby tree.

As the mob drew closer to the tree, a Regulator wearing a blue Army field jacket began tying a noose in a rope that had been thrown over the lowest limb of the tree.

From the crowd could be heard a voice identifying the woman. "It's the gambler William Burns' mistress!"

"That ain't nobody's mistress. That's jest another spic whore!" cried another voice.

The miner dragging the woman answered a question from the crowd. "I went there looking for my pardner—and she stabbed him to death, that's what she done!"

The woman hit at the man dragging her and her smock came open, as she screamed, "Filthy Anglo!" Fighting hands away from her smock, she yelled, "He broke into my house! He assaulted me!"

As she struggled to hold her smock together, one of the men yanked it open and it tore, exposing her abdomen and legs.

"Stop!" cried a man in a business suit who was carrying a black satchel in one hand.

They were under the tree now, and the Regulator, who was about to slip the noose over the woman's head, paused.

"I'm a doctor," the man stated, turning to face the mob.

"G'wan, string her up!" came a cry from the crowd.

"Give her a fair trial and hang her!" cried another voice.

"Quiet!" shouted the doctor. "I am a doctor and I

say that this woman is in no condition to be hanged!'' He glared at the men surrounding him and, in the moment's silence, explained, ''Because she is pregnant.''

The miners pushed the good doctor aside, drowning his protests with howling laughter, as the Regulator slipped the noose over the woman's head.

''Caro mio!'' the woman cried, reaching toward one section of the mob where a man was pushing and shoving, trying heroically to break through.

''It's the gambler, Burns,'' said one of the miners.

''She's his mistress,'' said another.

''Caro!'' the woman screeched. ''Save me!''

William Burns finally broke through the crowd and the woman tore free and rushed into his arms. He was a short man, about five feet, five inches in height, stocky and immaculately barbered and dressed. He wore a flannel suit edged in velvet ribbon, a black and gold brocaded weskit, and flowing satin tie. He tore the noose off the woman's neck, moved her behind him, and bravely faced the mob.

''You can't do this! It's uncivilized!'' he yelled at the men. ''I demand she get a fair trial before the *alcalde*!''

''She's already had a fair trial,'' said a Regulator, who had retrieved the noose and was holding it.

''You call this a fair trial!''

''John Murdock says she killed his partner. That's good enough for me.''

''Maybe she had just cause to kill him!'' yelled Burns, standing on tiptoe to appear taller.

''Ain't no just cause for a greaser to kill an American citizen,'' said the Regulator.

"Yeah, she's only a spic," said a voice from the crowd.

The Regulator went on, facing the gambler, Burns, but really talking to the crowd: "I say she's had her trial. Now what's the verdict, men?"

"Hang her! String her up!" cried the mob.

Strong, callused hands reached for the gambler, Burns, dragging him back through the crowd. Yelling and cursing, some of the men did their duty by kicking the gambler down the street while the others continued the hanging, their zealous shouts covering the last screams of the woman who, in a few moments, hung limp and naked from the hanging tree.

On the board sidewalk, in front of Shade's Saloon on Kearny Street, Captain Samuel Roberts and a group of his Regulators stood talking. Coal-oil lamps on each side of the saloon entrance, at the corners of the building, and illuminating the sign over the saloon made the night as bright as day.

Noisy conversation, shrill feminine laughter, and the tinny sound of an untuned piano came from the crowded room beyond the swinging doors.

Samuel Roberts, ever busy with his plans for power, was talking in a harsh, authoritative tone of voice to the four men grouped about him. In the lamp light, his long nose and lantern jaw showed a lineage of cockney descent. Clean-shaven, trim and neat in his officers' uniform, he looked the strong, powerful leader he intended to become.

A last few words, a final handshake, and Samuel Roberts started into the shadows and earthen wagon ruts of Kearny Street.

A *Chileno*, pushing a laden cart down the street, tried to stop it. Roberts pulled himself up abruptly. Too late; one of the cart wheels touched his uniform, leaving a smear of mud.

On the other side of Kearny Street, a young Mexican and his girl-wife were walking hand in hand, athrill with the excitement of the summer night, the joy of their youth, and the fullness of their young love.

As Roberts cursed and grabbed the *Chileno* and the group of Regulators came to his aid, the boy let go of the girl's hand and started toward them. The girl was quick and strong. She caught the youth, dragged him back, and forced him against the wall of the building and held him there, in the shadows, with her body pressed against him.

"Joaquín, no!" she whispered urgently.

"But Rosita—"

The girl's hand, slapped across his mouth, stopped further protest.

In the darkness of the street, two of the Regulators held the *Chileno* pinned against his cart as he jabbered in rapid Spanish his apology and plea for release. Cursing, Roberts brushed at the smear of mud on his uniform.

"Teach 'im a lesson, Capt'n!"

Roberts efforts to clean his uniform only made it worse. Anger mounting, he looked at the cringing *Chileno*, held between the two Regulators.

One man had his gun out. "Should I put a bullet in the dirty greaser, Capt'n?"

Roberts had control of his temper now. Thinking coolly, weighing how he, as their leader, could keep the respect of his men, and their loyalty too, he said,

"For an accident? No! Put that gun away, Bull."

As the man reluctantly holstered his gun, Roberts grabbed the knife from his belt. Then knocked off the Chileno's big hat and grabbed a handful of greaser hair in one hand and held it, while he cut off the foreigner's ears, first right, then left.

As the *Chileno*'s howls of fright and pain filled the night, Shade's saloon emptied as miners crowded through the doors out into the street to see the fun.

In the shadows across the street, Rosita hid her face in Joaquín's chest, but used all her strength to keep him pressed to the wall. The youth felt his stomach heave at the sight of violence and blood, felt a weakness sweep through his body, and put his arms about the girl to protect her and to steady himself.

PART I

Chapter 1

Clear and blazing sunlight shone over all the peaceful valley which comprised the holdings of Esteban Carillo in the state of Sonora, Mexico. A blue and cloudless sky arched incredibly high and wide. Down a two-mile slope of knee-high grassland, where bands of thoroughbred horses roamed free, could be seen the buildings and corrals grouped about the main house of the *hacienda*. The rising southern slope of the valley was a vineyard and fruit orchard. Farther up the valley, a great herd of cattle grazed in scattered clusters. Green and gold in the sun, it was a land of peace and abundance.

In front of the main house, there was a swarm of activity about three circus wagons which were being loaded. From a corral, Joaquín Carillo, youngest son of Esteban, led two magnificent horses, bred of the famous Isabella stock, brought from Spain in the year 1774, by Juan Palamino, an officer under Captain Juan Bautista Arizo, who led the first Mexican immigrants into California. These thoroughbred horses of beautiful form and golden coloring were commonly called Palaminos, after the man who had introduced them to the new world.

Following Joaquín, Rosita Felix, his wife of one month, led two more of the beautiful golden horses.

It was April 1849.

In that year Joaquín was nineteen, a slim, broad-shouldered youth, handsome of face and physique; a gentle man who had a way with horses and the same gentle way with family and friends. These were horses he had bred and trained, horses that responded to verbal and signaled commands as Joaquín and Rosita performed breathtaking acts in the circus ring.

Rosita was seventeen, a girl in years but a woman in all ways; a woman who had been in love with Joaquín, her husband of one month, from the time she was a child. A woman who loved horses because Joaquín loved horses. A woman who rode and performed with amazing skill and dexterity because Joaquín had trained her. A woman whose whole life and love was Joaquín.

She had the cameolike, perfect features of the Spanish aristocracy, from which her family was descended. Her ebony hair hung free and unbound in soft waves below her shoulders. Her hair, in a time when almost all women of Spanish blood bound their hair in tight buns or braids, was her husband's delight. He couldn't keep from touching it. Now Rosita wore a riding skirt. When they performed, she wore toreador pants and a bolero jacket, the same as Joaquín.

As Joaquín tied his two horses to rings at the rear of the first wagon, Rosita tied the two she led, with the same strong knots, to the back of the second wagon. Then laughing together, so much in love, they moved back to the corral, she with her arm about Joaquín's waist, he with his hand in her hair at the back of her neck. They tied two more horses to the back of the third wagon, which would be their home while touring with the circus. These were the performing horses; other horses drew the wagons.

Joaquín's older brother, Jésus, who was in charge of the circus troupe, was working at the first wagon with two men in their thirties who were cousins, sons of Esteban's brother, Raphael.

Jésus called to his younger brother, "Joaquín, if you can leave your bride for a moment, will you help Claudio load the trunks in your wagon?"

It was said in fun and the three men paused in their work of folding and stowing the bulky circus tent to laugh affectionately and, perhaps, enviously as they wiped sweat from their faces.

Joaquín grinned shyly. He touched Rosita in good-bye and walked to where a youth, his own age, who looked so much like him they could have been mistaken for twins, was lounging in the shade of the last wagon, surrounded by an assortment of packed trunks.

This was Claudio Carillo, youngest son of Esteban's brother, Raphael, who had been born the same month and year as Joaquín. He was the same height and build as was Joaquín, and resembled him closely except for the scattering of freckles and the greenish color of his eyes, where Joaquín's eyes were deep brown, almost black. The two cousins had grown up together, played together, worked, fought, ridden together. They were as close as brothers and loved one another like brothers.

Joaquín grasped Claudio's hand and yanked him to his feet and, with much joking and roughhousing, they loaded the trunks.

There was not much more to do. The wagons, glistening red and gold in the morning sun, made a beautiful sight. All the other members of the troupe were lined up in front of the three circus wagons, their open or covered wagons packed, the horses hitched or saddled, and ready to depart.

Jésus had been months in preparation for this departure and now, as Joaquín and Claudio hitched up the large draft horses that would pull the wagons, Jésus gave each wagon a final inspection. The performing horses stamped and moved restlessly. The draft horses stood stolid and patient, the bells of their harnesses tinkling lightly now and then, shining like polished gold in the bright sun. All was ready.

On the veranda of the *hacienda*, Esteban Carillo and his wife watched these preparations with a touch of sadness. It would be a quiet house for the next few months, but it would be good for the young people to be out in the world, meeting other people, performing, and enjoying the excitement of circus life. They would be back for the harvest season and it would be an invaluable experience for them all.

Behind Esteban stood the Felix family, Rosita's people. Beside Señora Carillo, stood Jésus' wife and two children, hand in hand, sad but smiling bravely to hide the melancholy of this parting. Below, at the foot of the steps leading up to the veranda, stood Esteban's brother, Raphael, and his plump and matronly wife, their faces revealing the same mix of emotions. And, around them, all the families of the other members of the troupe.

At the wagons, Jésus secured the last strap and signaled to the others. "It is finished, *bueno*? Let us say our goodbyes."

Excited and impatient, the troupe moved back to the big house. Esteban Carillo shook hands and hugged his two sons. Rosita and Señora Carillo clung together and wept. Raphael embraced his three sons and stood, with tears in his eyes, as they lined up to kiss their mother who was most brave until she kissed her youngest, Claudio.

"Vaya con Dios." She clung, weeping, embarrassing Claudio.

His two older brothers grinned at his discomfort until she gathered them also into her arms and wept over all three of her sons, as if they were marching off to war.

The Felix family had to, each of them, weep with Rosita and hug Joaquín. And Jésus kissed his wife and each child. And the other members of the troupe, all cousins or in-laws from somewhere in the family, were all kissing and hugging and weeping with each other. Until Esteban came down the steps of the veranda, gathering them all together, and spoke a prayer in Spanish, blessing them and the horses, to assure a successful trip and a safe return.

Finally, as the circus wagons moved out following the long line of other wagons and mounted men, Rosita looked back and blew a kiss to the clan gathered there in front of the big house. She burst into uncontrollable tears, although leaving to travel with Joaquín was what she wanted more than anything else in the world. Joaquín shifted the reins to his left hand and put his arm about her. He looked back over Rosita's head and waved, felt sadness, but the excitement within him was bubbling like new wine.

From the house, the wagons grew smaller as they moved down the road leading out of the valley, one behind the other, flashing glitters of red and gold in the shimmering sunlight. Silently, the families watched until the caravan looked like a file of toy wagons and horses, not real people but tiny dolls.

Two months later, after traveling as far north as San Francisco, with overnight stops at several of the larger settlements, the circus was in Monterey. The big tent, erected at the end of Monterey's main street, was illuminated with kerosene torches and held most of the town's population, seated on folding benches around the one ring where Joaquín and Rosita were performing.

Monterey, in that year, 1849, was a Spanish town, grown up around the Mission San Carlo de Borromeo de Monterey, established in 1770, at what was then the northern terminus of *el Camino Real*, the Royal Highway, which paralleled the Pacific coast from Loreta in Baja California. Monterey had been the capital of Alta California, and an important seaport under Spanish and Mexican rule. It was the city where Commodore John Drake Sloat, commander of the U.S. flagship, *Savannah*, first raised the American flag before the Treaty of Guadalupe Hidalgo gave Alta California to the United States. One week before the signing and ratification of that treaty, which ended the war with Mexico in 1848, gold had been discovered in the Coloma Valley above Fort Sutter.

Although California had become United States territory that year, there was as yet only a handful of American residents in Monterey; the Army officers and enlisted men who lived at the *presidio*, a few businessmen, storekeepers, traders and shipping merchants. So the audience was mainly Spanish-speaking.

Expressive and emotional, they loved the performance and the Mariani music played by four men of the troupe on guitar, trumpet, concertina and maracas, as Joaquín and Rosita in their tight pants and trim bolero jackets rode the golden horses around the ring, somersaulting into and out of the saddles, and doing other acrobatic feats astride and standing on the flanks of the graceful galloping mounts.

The music ended as the two performers leaped lightly to the ground and bowed to the enthusiastic applause. Then Joaquín lined the horses up behind them, and the two riders and six horses all bowed together. Applause thundered. Another signal and the horses filed from the ring, prancing and throwing their heads in response to the audience. And Joaquín and Rosita bowed again and again, taking all the credit for themselves, as they followed the beautiful horses out of the ring.

Outside, Joaquín hugged his partner and swung her around in joyous exhultation. Then stopped.

"What's this!"

All about them on the circus lot was confusion and frantic activity. Members of the troupe were taking down tents and packing their belongings. Everyone was talking excitedly. Claudio came running toward them, breathless.

"It's gold! GOLD!"

He grabbed them and pulled them toward a group of their people gathered beside Jésus' wagon. "Up north! They've found gold, Joaquín! It's in the rivers—in the creeks! All you've got to do is pick it up! GOLD!"

Claudio pushed through the crowd, dragging Joa-

21

quín with him. "Show him!" he yelled at a stranger in the center of the crowd.

Joaquín looked back for Rosita and reached one hand out to pull her up beside him. In the darkness, in the light of torches and cooking fires, Joaquín peered at the stranger, a man wearing a straw *sombrero* and *serape*, and knew he was not Mexican, but rather from Chile in South America. He looked around at the familiar faces of the members of the troupe and saw the wild excitement in their eyes and expressions.

Claudio was pulling his arm. "Miguelita brought him from the cantina. Listen to him, Joaquín. Look!"

He shouted at the stranger again, silencing the excited chattering of the crowd. "Show him! Show him the gold!"

The stranger shrugged affably. Smiling patiently, he emptied part of the contents of a small chamois sack into one hand and held it out for inspection.

Yellow lumps, irregularly shaped, some as big as acorns, glittered in the firelight.

"Tell him!" Claudio shouted.

The stranger shrugged again, good-naturedly. "Stanislaus," he said. "The whole river's full of them. Every creek flowing into it. The very ground you walk on—"

The excited shouting and talk of the troupe made it impossible to hear more. The young men wondered and speculated. The older men were skeptical. The women talked of a raven that had been seen playing with an infant of the troupe. An old crone said that an owl had rung the mission bells at midnight.

Joaquín looked around at the faces of these people he had known all his life. Cousins, in-laws, they were all strangers now, seized by the gold fever.

Suddenly, they quieted. Jésus was there examining what the *Chileno* held in his hand. Jésus took one of the yellow lumps, weighed it in his hand, then placed it on the iron rim of the wagon wheel and hit it with a rock. It flattened without cracking.

"It's gold!" he said. "It's the pure stuff!"

The men whooped and hollered. They hugged each other and joyously made plans to leave immediately.

Jésus wanted to know more. "What are they paying?" he asked the *Chileno*.

"Sixteen dollars an ounce."

Jésus judged the weight of the lump of gold. "Then this nugget's worth about eighty dollars?"

The *Chileno* shrugged, nodding agreement. The crowd roared. The men pounded each other, calculating the treasure they could amass before winter set in.

"How much gold is there to be found?" Jésus asked.

Shrugging again, the *Chileno* said, "It's everywhere. In the creeks. In the riverbed. In the banks of streams. Wherever there is water, there is gold. With closed eyes you could find it."

"Are there many others there seeking this gold?"

"Few stay over the winter," said the *Chileno*. "Now there are many moving in."

"Will you take us there?"

"No, *amigo*. All winter I have been there, freezing. I have all one man could ever need. I am going home."

On a map, the *Chileno* showed them where the Stanislaus River flowed into the San Joaquín Valley, where his strike had been located, and the general area of the lower gold fields.

Most of the crowd had dispersed to pack their belongings. Some were leaving immediately; others would leave in the morning. Jésus looked about at the members of his troupe and shook his head.

"This is the end," he said to Joaquín and the two cousins. "The circus is finished."

"What else?" said one of the cousins. "With gold to be picked up like stones on the ground. We are going too, no?"

Jésus nodded. "*Sí.* It is an opportunity we cannot pass by." He turned to his younger brother. "Joaquín, will you come with us?"

Joaquín hesitated. He looked at Rosita. This was his first big decision for the two of them. They had no need for gold. Their life was in Sonora. Their home was there, their families, his horses, and all the necessities of their life together. But gold for the taking . . . gold to be picked out of the streams . . . a fortune laying there to be carried off. In his own mind he was feeling the same excitement which had seized the others.

Rosita's eyes were downcast. Was the gold fever there, too? Can man ever read a woman's heart? He asked, "What do you want, my dove?"

She glanced up at him, and said, "I want only to be with you."

In that brief glance, Joaquín caught an unnatural excitement that matched his own feeling of recklessness and daring.

"We have no need for gold," he said.

"That is true, *caro mio.*"

"How would it benefit us?"

"In no way." Rosita's eyes were again downcast.

"Do you believe it is there?"

A shake of that midnight hair. "No."

"Nor do I," said Joaquín. "Let us go to see if it is true."

Rosita squealed with delight and hugged him around the neck. Jésus and the cousins grinned. Claudio whooped and caught them to him and the three of them danced there in a circle, holding hands and whooping with delight.

"*Bueno!*" said Jésus, "But first we must make plans. Joaquín, you will take your wagon and we will take ours. Claudio, you and one of the men will take the other wagon back home, with the palominos, the tent, and all the circus equipment. You tell the family of this news and bring back any who want to come."

He spread the map on a table and encircled an area of the Stanislaus River. "This is where we will be," he told Claudio. "In a month we will see you there. Come back with a good covered wagon and good horses, with all the food and tools you can bring. There will be a share for you in whatever gold we may find."

A rebellious Claudio glanced at his two brothers before replying. They both nodded. "The family should be informed," said one. "You go," said the other.

Claudio made no reply. He slammed his hat on the ground and walked away into the melee of the circus grounds.

Jésus said, "Already this gold gives us problems. I knew it would cause trouble."

"This is no problem," said one of the cousins. "Claudio will do as he is told. He is a good kid."

Chapter 2

Pitching and swaying, the two brightly painted circus wagons jolted along an almost invisible trail which paralleled the Stanislaus River. Last night they had camped at the mouth of the river, where it emptied into the San Joaquín. With morning light they had turned east, following the south bank of the twisting, flashing mountain stream toward its source. Bright sunlight dappled a virgin woodland awakening to spring. The trail they followed was little more than an occasional sign of hoofprints, or a faint wagon-wheel rut, where other gold seekers had gone in or come out of diggings located along this stream.

High on the wagon seat, Rosita clung to Joaquín's arm, to keep from being thrown off, as they careened over hidden rocks. The two draft horses plodded constantly onward, following the wagon in front on which rode Jésus and the two cousins.

"Such a land!" cried Joaquín, entranced by the mystery and abundance of the almost inpenetrable forest. Around a bend in the river, they had come upon a grassy sunlit meadow at the base of a waterfall, where wild horses were feeding. They had surprised deer drinking in the river, weasels sliding on the bank, foxes, rabbits, a lumbering bear. They had heard the cry of cougar deep in the shadows of the trees, seen whole wheeling flocks of mourning doves so numerous they darkened the sun, and listened to the myriad sounds of birdsong and tweetings in the woods surrounding them.

"But such a rough road," said Rosita, clinging.

"It is no road!" Joaquín cried exuberantly. "We are the first."

Rosita looked at him severely. They had passed others who had come before them; rough men in woolen shirts, with pants stuffed into high boots, who had wintered here and called to them from the stream bank where they panned or worked a roughly-built sluicing rocker. They were men eager to talk because they had been so long alone. Men who told unbelievable tales of strikes and lodes to be found elsewhere. Always elsewhere, not where their claim was staked.

The wagons were approaching a curve in the stream where shale had made a slight beach. Through the opening in the trees the sun could be seen setting on a distant ridge of the high Sierra Nevada mountains.

"Jésus!" Joaquín called. "Let us stop here for the night."

Jésus turned in his seat, looking back, then conferred with the two cousins, all nodding.

"Pull up," Jésus called and reined his wagon to a halt.

Joaquín drove his horses closer, set the brake of the wagon, and jumped down. Rosita followed, falling into his arms, and they rolled on the ground, tumbling and laughing.

27

Jésus and the cousins watched them for a moment, smiling affectionately at such an extravagance of young love, then they all got on with their work. The cousins unhitched the horses and led them to the water to drink. Jésus spread out his map to study it. As Rosita got food and cooking untensils from the wagon, Joaquín gathered firewood. Coming back with an armload of wood, he chose a place for the fire near the edge of the shale beach.

"This all right?" he called to Rosita, since she was the cook.

She glanced up from measuring beans into a pot and nodded.

He selected a heavy limb and placed it for a back-log upon which to build the fire. Then, before placing the kindling, he scraped a smooth place in the shale with his foot.

"LOOK! Jésus! Rosita! LOOK!"

They all stopped what they were doing. Joaquín was on his knees in the shale, scraping the earth. They rushed over.

"Look!" Joaquín pointed at the earth, at flashes of yellow stones, some like wheat kernels and some as big as acorns.

"It's *gold*!" he cried. He scooped up a handful of the shale, picked out a nugget, and handed it to Rosita. Then one to Jésus, and to each of the cousins.

"Gold!" He leaped up, caught Rosita, and dragged her over to where his brother and cousins were talking excitedly. "It's true! It is here! There's gold all over the place!"

The cousins were hugging and slapping Jésus and each other on the backs. Joaquín grabbed up one of the

28

pans Rosita had brought out of the wagon and waded into the water. He scooped up a panful of river bottom and swirled the water and lighter soil and gravel out. Then he yelled triumphantly.

Stomping back through the water, he showed them the pan. The sand and gravel in the bottom was flecked with yellow flakes and small grains of bright gold.

Unbelievable. Incredible. They yelled at each other, wildly excited, unable to believe their good fortune; that gold lay in the very ground they walked upon, all about them, everywhere, there for the taking.

"Madre de Dios!" Who could believe it? Jésus took off his hat and crossed himself. The cousins did the same.

Rosita recalled them all to reality. "Come, get the fire started. The beans can be cooking while you talk."

Wonderful woman. Child bride, yes, but a woman in all ways. Joaquín hugged her, laughing. He handed Jésus the pan of gravel and gold and picked up his kindling to start the fire.

After eating, they were too excited to sleep and sat around the campfire, talking and making plans, wondering who would come back with Claudio and how long it would be until they arrived. As darkness blacked out the forest, the sounds of nightlife, of the endless pursuit and flight for survival, were all about them. Beyond the circle of firelight, yellow eyes gleamed in the brush, a wild thing screamed in death throes, a cougar snarled a terrifying challenge, a night bird warbled a mating call.

Rosita pressed close to Joaquín. The cousins sat cross-legged, each with a rifle in his lap. The sky, spangled with stars, seemed to press upon the treetops. The silence, when it was unbroken, was like black velvet. And underfoot, and all about them, lay gold. They sat on gold. This night they would sleep on gold. The fire was melting gold as it burned lower.

Finally, Jésus designated the watch, two hours for each man, and they went to sleep.

Joaquín was so excited he could not sleep but, in the privacy and safety of their wagon, Rosita quieted him. "Hush. Just lie there and be still." And suddenly a cousin was shaking him. It was his watch, the last one of the night.

Outside the wagon, sitting with his back against a tree trunk, Joaquín handled the rifle gingerly. He was not sure he would know how to use it. So he laid it on the ground at his side and just sat there, thinking.

As his eyes adjusted to the darkness, he could make out shapes and shadows. The campfire still glowed with a cluster of red coals. The horses slept, with occasional stirrings, on the picket line. The stars, bigger and brighter than ever now in this hour before dawn, flashed reflections here and there in the river. The forest had grown quiet and the flowing water made a soft, soothing sound.

Wide awake, impatient for the day to begin, Joaquín fell in love with this wild, unspoiled land.

In love with this very place, between the river and the forest. It was so different from the wide, sunlit valley in which he had grown up. There was peace, what was known and familiar. There was security. There was home.

This was a land of excitement and danger. A land of challenge, with so many things to learn about its hostilities and about survival. A land that would demand much, but promised great rewards. The gold was part of it. But there was much more here: the abundance of nature, the dense forest, the variety of wildlife, the distant High Sierras, the rushing, twisting, changing river.

It was a land of plenty, but not of peace. It was a wild and adverse land. A land to be mastered like a wild horse, firmly but with gentleness and love.

Before dawn, he built up the campfire and, when it was roaring brightly, he roused Rosita by kissing her awake. Lying beside her in the wagon, while the others slept unguarded, they kissed and held each other and whispered words of love.

As she came fully awake, he asked, "Do you like it here, my little dove?"

She sat up and touched the side of his face. 'Wherever we are together, I like."

Kneeling beside her, he told her of his thoughts while on guard duty. "It is not just the gold," he said. "It's everything—the river, the forest, the hills. It's a new land, not like the land of our fathers which has already been conquered and subdued, and is handed to us for the taking. This is a land of challenge. A land we can make our own."

Rosita sensed his passion. She stood and pulled Joaquín to his feet. "My husband," she said, "whatever you feel for this place, I too feel. It is a beautiful land, a wonderful land. We will make it whatever you want."

What a woman! Joaquín grabbed her and would have made love to her right there, before breakfast, but she broke away, laughing.

"Later," she cried. "Now I make coffee and food for you men."

She leapt lightly from the wagon and busied herself at the fire which had burned down to a bed of glowing coals, just right for cooking. Joaquín went to awaken the others. It was not yet dawn.

As they broke their fast with tortillas, coffee, and bacon, Joaquín asked Jésus, "Are you going farther?"

"*Sí,*" said Jésus. "To Mormon Gulch where the *Chileno* advised us."

"How far is that?"

"Another twenty miles perhaps."

Jésus got the map and laid it on the ground between them, showing where they were and where they were going.

Joaquín studied the map, impressing it in his memory. Then he said, "We are going to stay here, my Rosita and I. This is where I first found gold. I claim it for us. And for you, too, if you don't like it where you go and wish to come back."

"We should stay together," said Jésus.

"Maybe you will be back," answered Joaquín. "But for me, I have come far enough. I love it here— this place. We go no farther."

Jésus glanced at the cousins. He shrugged his shoulders. They shrugged in return. It was settled.

Before they separated, one of the cousins offered Joaquín his rifle. "You should have a gun."

"No. You keep it. You will need it."

"But I have my pistol. We have several guns, you have none."

Joaquín laughed. "Hey, I don't even know how to shoot it."

"If you need it, you will know how to shoot."

Joaquín waved it away. "You know I don't hunt game. That I do not kill."

"Not for game." The cousin was serious. "To protect your life."

"No, no gun." Joaquín was adamant.

The cousin knew Joaquín was wrong, but he tossed the rifle back into their wagon and they said their goodbyes. The cousins hugged Joaquín and Rosita. Jésus kissed each of them on the cheek.

"We will be back to see you. You come and see us," he said.

And if you don't like it there, come back," said Joaquín. "There is room enough here for all of us."

"And gold enough for all," added Rosita.

They watched the wagon pull out. They waved as the wagon entered the deep cover of the forest. Then, as Rosita started to collect pots and pans, to clean up, Joaquín caught her hand.

"Wait."

He held her there as he glanced about the small open space between the shale beach of the riverbank and the encircling forest, to the distant ridge of hills eastward, where the sun had risen in flaming color. He looked across at the far bank of the river, which was about two hundred feet wide here, looked up and downstream at the flashing water, flowing gently here in this wide space, with only a few large boulders breaking the surface. He raised his eyes to the blue sky of morning and breathed deep of the brisk, dew-laden air.

Rosita watched him, saw the joy and satisfaction in his expression, and felt good.

Finally, Joaquín looked at her. "We should say a prayer," he said, "to ask God's blessing on this place, and on the house I will build you here, and the fine sons we will raise here."

Nodding agreement, tears of happiness in her eyes, Rosita knelt beside him there on the earth of this new land; she was so much in love with this good and gentle man who was her husband, it seemed she could not contain it all.

Chapter 3

The days passed, days full of work and plans.

Mornings Joaquín and Rosita panned the riverbed and raked the gravel and shale of the beach, searching for gold. After the midday meal and *siesta*, they explored the surrounding forest, up and down the river, looking for new diggings, getting to know the lay of this new land that would be their home.

Joaquín began clearing an area beyond the beach where he planned to build a log house and plant a bean crop. Each day they added to their sizable gold horde, which they kept in a trunk in the wagon.

It was about two weeks after they arrived that they were awakened from their *siesta* by the sound of voices. On the other bank of the river, four men were wading in the water, panning for gold. Evidently they liked what they found, because they started to hoot and holler joyfully and pound each other on the back.

Joaquín walked to the river's edge and called a greeting to them. They waved and called back, then one of them started across. The Stanislaus River was not deep here; in the deepest place it came only to the armpits of the man. He came up on the shale beach, stomping and shaking himself. He grinned and extended his wet hand.

He was surprised to see Rosita was a woman and he tore off his hat as he shook hands with Joaquín.

"Howdy, pardners!" he said, smiling broadly, and bowing slightly to Rosita. "I didn't know . . . seeing you from over there in them britches." He pointed to Rosita's toreador pants, her circus costume, which she had been wearing because they gave her more freedom than a skirt.

"*Buenas tardes,*" said Joaquín. "This is my wife."

The dripping miner bowed again. "Nice to meet you, ma'am. Good to see a lady," he said. "Ain't seen a lady since we left Frisco more'n a month ago." He turned to Joaquín, grinning, and slapped him on the shoulder. "And they ain't all ladies up there. Know what I mean?"

Joaquín nodded briefly to show he was not offended.

"Name's Harvey. Me and my pardners are going to camp here awhile." He pointed over to the men on the other bank. "You don't mind, do you?"

"We do not own the river," said Joaquín. "Our claim is here." He pointed to the area of beach which he had staked at each end. "And back into the woods."

Harvey looked around and saw the circus wagon, the pile of cut logs, and the cleared land. He was a stocky, grizzled man of about forty, his face tanned and weather-beaten and covered with stubby whiskers. He extended a powerful right arm, indicating the cleared land.

"Looks like you're planning to stay. Must have a good strike."

"It is not the gold," said Joaquín. "We love this land."

Harvey glanced up at Joaquín who was a head taller than he. "Well, some do . . . some don't. We're just after gold. We'll be here awhile, then be moving on."

As he started to leave, Rosita said, "Mr. Harvey, would you and your friends have supper with us tonight?"

Harvey turned and removed his hat again. "Why, that's right kindly of you, ma'am." He smiled broadly. "We're all kinda sick of our own cooking. A woman's cooking would taste mighty good to us—even if it is spic food."

He caught himself, looked up at Joaquín. "No offense meant."

"There is no offense," said Joaquín. "We are Mexican. And proud of it."

"Why, sure," said Harvey. Then he said to Rosita, "And I do thank you, ma'am."

"You're most welcome," said Rosita. "My husband will call you when it's ready, before sundown."

"Thank you, ma'am."

He started away again, and Joaquín said, "You can cross upstream without getting wet. There's a log across."

Harvey changed direction, moving up the beach, backing away from them, saying, "Thank you," and again, "Thank you, ma'am."

They watched until Harvey rejoined his partners on the other bank and waved back when the four men all waved across to them, calling out hearty acceptance of the dinner invitation.

• • •

A week or ten days passed without incident.

Joaquín and Rosita could see their neighbors' fire at night, or hear an occasional whoop when one of them discovered a special prize. The four partners could hear the ring of Joaquín's axe as he felled trees each afternoon. From time to time, they called a greeting back and forth across the river.

Joaquín felt no alarm. Rosita felt good about having other human beings nearby, in this wilderness.

Then one day, as they were eating their noon meal, they saw another man join the four partners. Idly, they watched as the men stopped work to greet the newcomer, who wore some kind of military uniform. They finished their meal, Rosita cleaned the dishes, and they retired to the wagon for a *siesta*.

Across the river, the men were drinking whiskey, laughing and joking, and bragging of the rich claim they were working.

The newcomer was Samuel Roberts. These four men were of the Regulators whom Roberts had commanded in San Francisco.

"Sure as hell good to see you, Capt'n," said Harvey.

Sam Roberts opened another bottle and took a drink. "Good to see you too, Harvey," he said. "And good to see you, John Little." He slapped the tallest man on the back and passed the bottle to him. "And you, Christian. And you, too, Bull Dutton. I told you I'd join up with you, didn't I?"

"That you did, Capt'n."

They all had another drink out of the new bottle and listened to the news of San Francisco. Sam Roberts brought two more bottles out of his saddlebags, and they sat there drinking and talking. Nobody bothered to build a fire and cook, not while a bottle was handy. They started to get boisterous and flushed with courage and camaraderie, as they talked of old times when the Regulators had terrorized San Francisco in the guise of law and order. They reminisced about when the captain had led them on raids against the helpless Chinese and on forays to pillage and rape among the Spanish-speaking harlots of Telegraph Hill.

The ring of Joaquín's axe and the smell of beans and coffee came across the stream as Rosita prepared the evening meal. This caught Sam Robert's attention.

"Who's the two men across the creek?" he asked.

Harvey laughed and slapped his thigh. "That's what we thought, too, Capt'n. But that little one in the britches is a woman. They're man and wife."

They all howled at the look of surprise Roberts gave them.

"They's greasers," said John Little.

"Yeah, but good folks," said Harvey. "They're real nice and friendly. That little gal's as pretty as one of them Chinee gals. And a good cook, too. Yeah, she fed us the first day we came."

"Must have a good strike," said Roberts, "or he wouldn't be chopping down trees to build a cabin."

"That I don't know," replied Harvey. "The guy's just a kid. He said they love this land. They're gonna squat there, I guess."

"They's greasers," said John Little.

"They got no right here," said Sam Roberts. "They're getting gold that should be ours."

"They was here first, Capt'n," said Harvey.

39

"No damn greaser's got a right to squat on American soil," said Roberts, eloquent with whiskey. "Next thing, they'll be putting up fences and telling us we can't cross over their land. They'll bring in other greasers. First thing you know, they'll claim the whole river. I say any gold in that river is American gold, for us Americans, not for no foreigners."

"Aw, Capt'n, we just took over California from Mexico last year. We're the foreigners, not them."

"You gotta stop talking like that, Harvey. Where's your patriotism? By god, I volunteered to fight for the stars and stripes and I'm gonna do it." Roberts turned to the others. "I say the gold in that river's American gold. What do you say, men?"

"The Capt'n's right!" John Little stood up and had to brace himself because his head was spinning. He passed the bottle to Christian and snapped to a wobbly salute. "I say the Capt'n's right. Let's get the gold."

"That's a stout fellow!" cried Roberts. "Bull Dutton, where do you stand—and you, Christian? Are you for the United States, or for them greasers?"

Christian took a last swallow, emptying the bottle, and nodded as he gulped and choked on the whiskey. Bull Dutton sniffed the southerly breeze, bringing the odor of beans and bacon across the stream. "Yeah, I'm with yuh, Capt'n. And maybe we'll get some grub while we're over there, too."

"Good men!" cried Roberts. He stood up, straightened his uniform, and took command. "Get your guns," he ordered, "and we'll drive off them dirty greasers across the creek."

"Aw, now, wait a minute." It was Harvey, the voice of reason. "They ain't hurtin' nobody."

"Harvey, it's our gold they're gettin'." said Roberts.

"We been doing all right. There's enough gold here for all."

"There'll be more for us if we drive them off."

"It ain't right, Capt'n," argued Harvey.

"They's greasers," said John Little. "That makes it right. Lead on, Capt'n."

"This way, Capt'n," said Bull Dutton, starting upstream toward the log crossing.

"Let's go, men!" Capt'n Roberts brandished his pistol. He grabbed Harvey by the arm and pulled him along, saying, "Come on, Harvey. Stick with your pardners and get your share."

They staggered drunkenly through the brush, then sobered somewhat when Christian fell off the log into the water. On the other side, they crept in single file behind their captain as they approached the bright circus wagon.

Joaquín and Rosita were just sitting down to eat when Sam Roberts stopped behind a tree at the edge of the clearing to organize his attack. Christian, who was last in line and still trying to shake himself dry, ploughed into Bull Dutton, who lost his balance and crashed into Harvey, and all three of them fell in a thrashing heap.

At the sound of the commotion, Joaquín and Rosita looked around, saw the men who were their neighbors from across the stream, and Joaquín stood and started forward to greet them.

Using this moment of surprise with true military dispatch, Sam Roberts leaped from behind the tree, grabbed Joaquín, and jammed his pistol into Joaquín's throat.

At the same time, he yelled, "John, get the woman."

John Little caught Rosita and struggled to hold her. Joaquín began to fight. He wrestled the gun away from his throat and threw Roberts to the ground.

"Christian! Bull!" Roberts cried for help. "Get this wildcat off me!"

By this time the other three men had scrambled to their feet and charged into the camp. Christian and Harvey pinned Joaquín to the ground.

"You all right, Capt'n?"

"Yes, I'm all right. Get some rope and tie that bastard to a tree."

"Yes, sir, Capt'n. Just hold him there till I quiet him," said Christian. He took a heavy log from the stack of firewood and smashed it down on Joaquín's head.

"Good!" Sam Roberts stood up, brushing himself off. He looked over at Rosita who was screaming and screeching Spanish invective at them all. "Shut her up," he said, and John Little slammed a fist into her jaw.

It did not knock her unconscious, but it did quiet her and John Little sat on the ground, still holding the girl, running his hands over the girl's body.

Roberts looked about, assessing his position. Christian and Harvey were tying Joaquín to a tree. Bull Dutton was sitting at the table, wolfing beans and biscuits.

"Bull! What are you doing!" Roberts bellowed.

"I'm eatin', that's what."

"Well, stop eating and look for the gold."

"When I'm finished, Capt'n."

Then Roberts saw John Little fondling the girl and yelled, "What the hell are you doing, John Little!"

Rosita was groggy but fighting to stay conscious, to resist. John Little had her blouse open and was feeling her breasts. Feebly, she tried to restrain him as he tore the blouse off and slipped her petticoat down to her waist. He looked up at Sam Roberts, grinning idiotically.

"I'm gonna get me a piece of this, Capt'n."

"We're here for gold!" yelled Roberts. "Get the gold!"

"Sure, Capt'n, when I finish."

He unbuttoned and tore the toreador pants off Rosita and tried to lay her out on the ground but she struggled, stronger now, resisting him. Finally he took his belt and strapped her hands together behind her back, then knelt between her legs and dropped his pants to his knees and opened his red underwear.

Christian had been in the wagon and now came toward the table with a bottle in each hand. Roberts stood beside the table, still arguing with Bull Dutton.

"Look, we got tequila!" cried Christian. "That goes good with beans, Bull." He handed Bull one of the bottles.

"Did you find the gold?" Roberts wanted to know.

"Forget the gold, Capt'n." He opened the other bottle. "Here, have a drink. Let's eat first. We got all night to find the gold."

He took a swig of the bottle and began eating the other plate of beans on the table. With a biscuit in one hand, the bottle in the other, he asked, "Why don't you sit down, Capt'n? Enjoy yourself." Then, seeing John Little floundering atop Rosita, Christian slapped Bull Dutton good-naturedly.

"Bull, look at John!" he howled. "Don't that beat all! Hey, I'm gonna get me some of that when he gets off!"

Bull Dutton looked around. He saw the floundering stop as Rosita heaved her assailant off and out of her body, and the two of them lay quiet and spent for the moment. Bull stood, wiping his mouth with the back of his hand, and hitched up his pants.

"After me, you are." He slapped Sam Roberts on the back and pushed him toward the table. "Sit down, Capt'n. Get some of them beans. They're real good."

Bull walked over to Rosita, knelt between her legs, and started to undo his belt buckle. She started to kick and scream. He stopped working at his belt buckle, grasped her shoulders, and lifted and slammed her head on the ground. Again and again, he banged Rosita's head on the shale and rocks of the beach, until she ceased struggling and was silent.

He glanced around at the men at the table as he loosened his belt and dropped his pants. "I don't like all that noise when I'm fuckin'," he explained.

Christian laughed through a mouthful of beans. Samuel Roberts looked around at his command: John Little stretched out on the beach, recovering, Bull Dutton pumping away atop the girl, Christian stuffing himself with food and drink. He shook his head in disgust and, like a good commander, adjusted his strategy to meet the situation. He took a drink of tequila and was about to sit down when Joaquín started to come alive.

Yells, screams, and threats came from the man tied to the tree as he struggled against his bonds.

Roberts set the bottle on the table and walked to the tree. All the frustration he felt with his men, who were more concerned with their appetites than with finding the gold, he took out on the helpless man tied to the tree. He punched and punched, right and left into body and face, until Joaquín sagged against his ropes in unconsciousness.

Roberts rubbed his knuckles as he walked away from the tree and the inert body tied there. A smirk of satisfaction was on his face as he lifted the bottle and looked over at Bull Dutton who was now standing over the unconscious girl, pulling up his pants and buckling his belt.

Roberts set the bottle back on the table. "You're right, men," he said. "Christ, see if you can find any more of this booze. We'll get their gold tomorrow. Let's enjoy ourselves for now."

"Attaboy, Capt'n!"

Roberts unbuckled his pistol and laid it on the table. He took a swallow of the tequila and said, "I'm gonna get myself a little of that Spanish ass, then have some of those beans. They look real good."

"Attaboy, Capt'n!" Christian cried again. "You go to it! Then I'm next!"

They took turns on Rosita. Whenever she recovered enough to fight back they beat her into submission. For a while, Joaquín regained consciousness and they let him watch his wife being ravished, then Roberts tired of that and quieted him by cracking his head with the butt of a pistol.

It was a good party. As night closed in, they fell

asleep, one at a time, wherever they sat or lay, satiated with food and liquor and sex.

Harvey awakened first. Some foraging raccoons knocked a tin plate off the table and it hit him in the face. He sat up, held his head, and looked about. It was daylight. He lay back again, but his head hurt more lying down than it did sitting up. He pushed up again, got onto hands and knees, and crawled to the stream and splashed water in his face and over his head.

He stood drying his face on his shirttail and looked about again. His partners lay sleeping, sprawled all over the place. Rosita lay naked and unconscious, her face bruised and swollen, her pubic hairs and crotch smeared with dried blood. Joaquín hung limp in his bonds against the tree.

Harvey shook his head to clear it. He squeezed his eyes and temples with both hands for a moment. He looked again and saw the same damning sight.

Unsteadily, he walked to Rosita, knelt, and slapped her face gently. She stirred. He collected her clothes and, as gently as he could, he dressed her. During this she stirred and murmured, but did not come fully awake.

Then he went to the tree and undid the ropes. Joaquín fell to his knees and came awake. Struggling to his feet by clawing at the tree, Joaquín grabbed at Harvey and began to fight him feebly.

"Now, none of that," Harvey growled as he caught Joaquín's hands and led him to Rosita, supporting the youth as they walked.

Joaquín knelt beside Rosita, lifted her shoulders, and clutched her face to his breast. He felt her stir and looked at her. She opened her eyes, tried to smile at

46

him, then closed her eyes as her head rolled back. Joaquín let her body lay back on the ground again, exhausted by the effort of holding her.

On all fours, leaning over her, he looked up at Harvey with such an expression of hatred that his bloody, bruised face was contorted into a mask of evil.

Harvey had to look away. He pressed his own throbbing head with one hand, then shook it sadly. ''I know,'' he said, looking down at the battered youth. ''It's unforgivable. You'll never forget. I ought to shoot you both, right now, because someday you'll come back and kill us.''

Joaquín's blazing eyes closed for a moment. He hung his head, saying softly, ''She fed you.''

''I know. I know.'' Harvey lifted Joaquín to his feet. Together, they lifted Rosita, who murmured and resisted until she looked about startled, saw Joaquín, and clung to him.

''Come on, get out of here before they wake up.'' Harvey pushed Joaquín toward the trees. ''They got more sense than I have. They'll shoot you dead if they see you.''

He walked with them, supporting Rosita, until Joaquín was stronger and could keep the girl from falling. Then he let them go. ''Just keep going,'' he said.

He watched a moment as they staggered away, then hollered, ''Just keep away from us. Go back to Mexico!''

Then he walked back to the camp. He started a new fire on the old ashes, searched through the wagon until he found coffee, flour, and bacon, and started cooking.

The smell of food aroused his partners. One by one they awakened, feeling miserable and looking worse.

With the first sips of hot coffee, they came back to life.

"Where's them greasers?" Sam Roberts wanted to know.

Harvey kept his face in his coffee cup. He took a big swallow. It tasted like bile.

"Yeah, where's them greasers?" asked Bull Dutton. "That little gal was a good cook."

"You were up first, Harvey," said Roberts.

Harvey looked at his captain. Roberts had started it all with his greed for gold. But it had been his partners, too. And he, himself. They were all weighed with the same amount of guilt.

Looking down at the ground, he said, "Must have got away in the night."

"We shoulda killed them damn spics, Capt'n," said Christian.

"You want we should go find them, Capt'n?" asked John Little. "They couldn't of got very far . . . not in the condition they was in."

Roberts thought about it. His head ached from the tequila. The coffee burned his tongue. He made a hasty, bad decision.

"No," he said. "Forget them. Let's find their gold."

Chapter 4

Getting a late start, but with Samuel Roberts now in command, they found the gold cache Joaquín and Rosita had kept in their trunk in the wagon. Weighing and dividing it made them forget their hangovers and, after some more coffee, they staked an enlarged claim on both sides of the river and started to work.

"You men keep your guns strapped on," Roberts ordered. "If that greaser comes back, kill him."

That made good sense and, although the gun was a hindrance while working, they followed their captain's order.

Christian and Bull Dutton worked the far side of the river. John Little, Harvey, and Sam Roberts worked the side where Joaquín and Rosita had established their claim. The camp settled down to a typical mining operation, as if last night had never happened. It was a rich claim and there were many occasions for rejoicing as one of them panned up an extra large nugget, or dug into an unusually heavy deposit of placer gold in the riverbank. As the sun climbed higher, flooding the clearing with green and gold light, reflecting bright flashes on the water, the men rolled up their sleeves and sweated out the last traces of tequila.

A massive grizzly bear came crashing through the underbrush upstream to drink, looked at them unafraid, then went lumbering off to find a more private spot. Deer and antelope could be seen occasionally in the cover of the forest or on distant slopes, but no one wanted to hunt fresh meat while there was gold to be found in each new pan or shovelful of earth.

Raccoons frolicked boldly at the fringe of the wood, drawn by the memory of the food they had scavenged there last night.

"Hey, lookee at them ring-tailed cats," John Little cried as they were eating their evening meal. He pointed at a group of three kittens tumbling and clawing at each other while a full-grown raccoon stood nearby, watching the camp patiently.

Harvey tossed a biscuit toward them, but the sudden movement startled the animals and they vanished.

The slope of pine and scrub oak across the river was spotted with the pink of laurel and the beginning spikes of purple lupine. Poppy, growing in a small clearing upstream, made a mass of brilliant orange. Birds chattered in the forest; thrasher, magpie, and finch. A blue jay flashed bright color in the undergrowth of manzanita at the edge of the clearing.

As the sun sank, the men gathered closer to the fire, healthily tired from the day's work and relaxed with a bellyful of food. No sign of last night's brutal orgy remained. No mention was made of it. It was a thing best forgotten.

But their captain did not forget. "We'll post a guard tonight," Sam Roberts ordered. "I don't want no sneaky greasers coming in here and taking our gold." What he left unsaid was that their lives were at stake as long as they remained here, with Joaquín and Rosita at large.

In the light of a kerosene lantern, he cleared a place on the table and began shuffling a deck of cards. "Any of you men want to try your luck before we turn in?"

For days Joaquín and Rosita staggered through the brush and undergrowth along the south bank of the river, traveling eastward, following an almost invisible trail, marked only by an occasional hoofprint or wagon-wheel rut. When Rosita could walk no farther, he carried her on his back until he was exhausted. Then they would rest or sleep. If it was daylight when Joaquín awakened, he would rouse Rosita and force her to go on. If it was night, they would stay where they lay until first light.

They had no food and became weaker as time went by. The water of the Stanislaus kept them alive and gave them direction. It was along this river the Jésus and the cousins were camped.

Joaquín lost count of the days. Rosita could no longer walk and he could carry her only a short distance before having to stop and rest. But he kept going, knowing that help was ahead, that Jésus would be there at the end of the trail, somewhere farther along this stream.

Five days later, carrying Rosita in his arms because he could no longer lift her up to his back, he struggled into an open place in the forest where a smaller stream joined the Stanislaus. He heard a shout and lifted his head to see one of the cousins sloshing through the water, running toward him, and he sank to the ground, his body falling over Rosita's, and passed out.

Far off, he could hear voices, felt himself being carried, being laid on something soft. *Gracias a Dios*, his mind offered a prayer of thanksgiving. Thank you, *Madre de Dios*.

The harsh burning of brandy in his throat brought Joaquín awake. He opened his eyes to see Jésus bending over him, forcing the liquor into his mouth. He swallowed, felt it burn his throat and revive his senses.

"Rosita?" he said weakly.

He turned his head to where Jésus was pointing and saw one of the cousins supporting Rosita in a sitting position on a straw pallet beside him, and holding a small glass to her lips.

"Ah . . ." He breathed a sigh of relief, closed his eyes, and would have sunk back to sleep.

Jésus shook him gently. "No. You must eat." He held Joaquín in a sitting position. "Take this. It will nourish you."

The other cousin held a bowl near his face and a spoon to his lips. Joaquín opened his mouth and swallowed. It was a hot meat broth.

"Ah, *bueno*." The cousin smiled sadly as he spooned more of the hot liquid into Joaquín's mouth.

Joaquín ate until the bowl was empty. He saw Rosita was being fed, too. He realized that they were inside a log cabin, each on a soft pallet, safe at last with his own people.

He closed his eyes and lay back. There was a pillow under his head, a blanket being pulled over him. As he sank into sleep he heard Jésus say, "Sleep now, *hermanito*, little brother. In a few hours you must eat more."

Later, Joaquín came awake, struggling to free himself from ropes that bound him to a tree. He gave a mighty heave, burst his bonds asunder, and found himself sitting in a darkened room. The door stood open to bright sunlight and he saw it was a windowless log cabin. Rosita lay beside him, sleeping quietly, her head on a pillow and covered with a blanket. Memory came flooding back, and relief; that they had found Jésus, that they had survived the ordeal.

He pushed up and knealt over Rosita and his head began to spin with weakness. When it steadied, he touched his lips lightly to her hair, pulled the blanket up snug around her throat, and tried to stand.

The room spun. He staggered to the wall and leaned against it until the spinning stopped. He stood there breathing deeply, flexing his arms and hands. Every part of his body was bruised and sore. His face was stiff. It pained when he opened his mouth. His chest hurt when he breathed. His head ached with a jarring, throbbing beat. He touched it and felt a large tender lump where the pistol butt had hit him.

Stronger now, he moved along the wall to the doorway. He leaned against the doorframe, squinting into sunlight. The dazzle of bright light hurt his eyes until they adjusted and he could make out the forest beyond the clearing of the camp, the sparkle of sunlight on water, the surrounding hills.

In the center of the camp a fire burned under a kettle suspended from a tripod. Beyond it was a rough table and benches. Down at the water's edge, where this smaller stream fed into the Stanislaus River, Jésus and the two cousins were working at a sluice. He started toward them.

Concentrating on where he was stepping, because

his head was still light, he heard a shout. He stopped, saw Jésus throw aside his shovel and come splashing through the water toward him.

He caught Joaquín by the shoulders. "*Hermano!* You should not be up." He started him back toward the cabin. "I thought you'd sleep all day."

Joaquín resisted him. "No! We must go back. Right away. Those men—those *Americanos*—"

Jésus led him to a bench at the table. Forced him to sit down. "Listen to me, *hermanito*. You go nowhere until you get your strength. You're up and awake, that's good. You have no broken bones, that's good. Now you sit there and you'll eat."

He went to the kettle over the fire and brought back a plate of steaming food. It was a corn meal and venison gruel.

The smell of it gave Joaquín stomach pangs. He hadn't realized how hungry he was. "No! We must go back—" he began.

"Quiet! You eat!"

Jésus handed him a spoon. He lifted a lid from a pan on the table and broke off a piece of biscuit and put it beside Joaquín's plate.

"But I've got to go back," Joaquín tried again.

"Don't talk. Eat!"

The smell was irresistible. Joaquín tasted the gruel. Delicious. He began to gulp it down.

"Slowly," said Jésus, touching his hand. "That is all for now. You will have more at supper. When you finish this, go back to sleep."

Joaquín watched him walk back to the sluice and begin working. He sat there and ate the food and could feel his strength returning. He looked about. The log cabin was built into the side of a hill. Its sod roof looked like part of the slope. The circus wagon was parked beside it and beyond the wagon was a small corral in which the two draft horses moved restlessly. The three men working together had accomplished much more than he had been able to do alone.

As he sat there, the food warm in his belly, the sun warm on his back, his eyes began to close. He stood, much steadier now, and walked back to the cabin. Inside, he lay down on the pallet beside Rosita, who was still sleeping.

Tomorrow he would go back, he thought as he pulled the blanket up over himself. Tomorrow . . .

"But it is our gold, Rosita's and mine. We found it. We worked for it."

"It is not worth dying for, little brother."

"It is those men who should die, those *Americanos*. What they did to my Rosita . . . I don't know how I can ever live with myself, how I can face my wife, my little dove, if I do not kill them."

"And how will you kill them? You, who don't even know how to shoot a gun, who never used a knife, who could not even help at slaughtering the pigs? *Madre de Dios*, how can such a chicken as you kill four men? You couldn't kill four sheep."

"Tell me, how can I do it, Jésus?"

"You can't! If you go back they will only kill you."

"But *we* could do it. You, me, the cousins, the four of us together. You know how to shoot the gun."

"Little brother, I would die for you, *sí*. We would all die for you. But what would that gain? Joaquín, you must realize we are a gentle people, we Mexicans.

55

Emotional, yes. We scream and weep, but we do not kill.

"These *Americanos* are different. They are fierce fighters. They are trained to kill. They are terrible with their guns and they shoot like devils. They rob and steal from us. They violate our women. They take our country and would drive us out. It is all wrong, but we cannot fight them. Even our armies cannot stand against them. Joaquín, you cannot hope to win what Mexico has already lost."

"But I must avenge my Rosita—"

"Better it is forgotten. Thank God, you are both still alive. Rosita does not want you to go back there to die for her honor. You think she wants to be a widow when you have not yet been married long enough for her to be a mother?"

"You reason well, Jésus, and your judgment is sound. I must agree with you. But how do I live with this shame? Every time I look on the woman I love, every time I see another *gringo* . . ." Joaquín covered his face with his hands to hide his burden of guilt. "Oh, why didn't they kill me?" he murmured.

Jésus shrugged, the age-old gesture of accepting what cannot be changed. Was there any other answer?

They were sitting at the rough table after breakfast the following day. Joaquín had told them all that had happened and asked their advice. The cousins could give no advice and had gone to start their day's work at the sluice. Rosita was still asleep, inside the cabin.

In all that broad spread of river valley there was nothing but peace and the blessings and harmony of a bountiful God. Sunlight bathed all the surrounding hills, flashing on crystal waters, feeding leaf and blade, penetrating the depths of the forest with shafts of liquid gold on fern and mossy bank, on blue fleeting wings and sleeping wildcat. And, wherever water flowed in this land of natural abundance, there was the hidden treasure of real gold for the finding and taking.

"Better they had killed me. I would rather be dead."

"No, *hermanito*, it is better to be alive. We will be on guard in case those *Americanos* come here. And we will fight them as best we can—like sheep fighting the wolves—but to go back there for revenge is senseless."

"But our wagon . . . our circus costumes . . . our horses . . . the gold we dug . . . the logs I chopped . . . I was going to build a house, live in this land, raise a family."

Jésus stood up. "Go ask Rosita, your little dove. Ask her if she wants to be your widow," he said, and started toward the riverbank.

Joaquín watched him go. The sun was warm on his back, the air was spiced with pine and woodsmoke, the strength was back in his young body, and life was sweet. It could be so sweet.

Chapter 5

Rosita ate a good supper that night. She was fairly recovered. The sleep and food had restored her. She had bathed and combed her hair and wore a clean linen shirt one of the cousins had given her. It was too big, but with the sleeves rolled up it would do until her own things were washed and dry. She also wore a pair of Jésus' trousers, rolled up at the bottoms.

In the light of the campfire, her face, bruised and swollen, was shiny with an unguent Jésus had rubbed on it. She was quiet and remote. She and Joaquín had not yet had a chance to talk, except for a few tender kisses and reassurances. Her mind had not yet absorbed all that had happened. Her thoughts still recoiled from those horrid, nightmarish memories.

Sitting at the table across from her, his back to the fire, his face in shadow, Joaquín's heart bled when he looked at her. His Rosita, his little dove. His mind writhed in shame, the food gagged in his throat, when he looked at her slim, dainty hands, her delicate bruised features, the baggy shirt covering her lovely body, that precious midnight hair.

He forced himself not to look at her. This desecrated

flesh, this body of virgin purity that had been entrusted to him, one man, with love and devotion and holy reverence. Despoiled. Ravished. Violated. His soul burned in torment. His mind seethed. His thoughts were crazy. Better it would have been if a grizzly bear had attacked her and eaten her before his eyes. If his horses, that he loved so much, had trampled her into a mass of bloody pulp. If the river had swallowed her and buried her in its treasure of hidden gold.

He sat there, struggling to hold his raging thoughts under control. He ate, forcing the food down. He needed strength, not reason; might, not sanity; vengeance, not logic.

In the gold fields, the miners work until dark. Each daylight hour is counted in ounces gained, or lost. With evening and darkness, they take time to cook and eat, then quickly retire, exhausted by the back-breaking labor, their constantly cold and wet feet, the excitements or sorrows of the day.

About eight o'clock the sun had set. By ten o'clock everyone was deep in sleep. Three straw pallets in the cabin; Joaquín on one, Jésus slept on another, with Rosita sleeping between them. The cousins had given their beds to Joaquín and Rosita and were sleeping in the circus wagon. Joaquín raised himself on one elbow. Rosita, at his side, breathed deep and slow. Jésus, on the far pallet, was snoring.

Joaquín reached under his pillow and his hand closed on the grip of a revolver he had secretly taken from the cousins' wagon earlier in the day. He pushed it under his belt. Then slid from his blanket and stood, crouching, listening for any change in the others' breathing. He felt in the darkness for his boots, picked them up, then moved slowly to the open door.

Outside, he looked about at the star-studded sky, the dying glow of the campfire, the starlight reflections on the water. He breathed deep. Never had he felt so alive, so awake, so vital.

Carrying his boots, stepping cautiously, he moved past the open back door of the wagon, heard the snoring of the cousins inside. At the corral he pulled on his boots, opened the gate, and went in. One of the horses moved forward, recognizing him.

He took it by the halter, talking to it in whispers, as he led it out, around the edge of the campsite, and across the small stream. On the other side he looked back. All he could see was the spot of orange firelight and the bulk of the circus wagon. The log hut and corral blended into the shadow of the hill. All he loved and held dear, his very reason for being, was over there, locked in the shadows.

He kept the horse quiet. He felt the revolver in his belt. It gave him some reassurance, but not much. He had no plan, but to go back there. God help him; but he had to go. The river would guide him through the night and the horse would get him there by morning.

Standing in the darkness, he crossed himself and offered a silent prayer. What would happen when he got there, God only knew. If they killed him, so be it. Death would be better than a life of shame. But he had to go.

Patting the horse on the neck, he leaped onto its back and kicked his heels into its sides.

It was full daylight before Joaquín began to recognize some landmarks that indicated he was within a few miles of his old claim. Soon he dismounted and walked on foot, the horse following along as he moved silently toward the camp.

As he came to the spot where the deadfall made a crossing of the river, he heard the voices of the *Americanos*. He stopped. He took the gun from his belt and moved forward cautiously. The good horse followed. He tried to make it stay but had no rope or way to tether it, so he moved on, the horse right behind him.

He caught a glimpse of bright red and gold. It was the circus wagon. He crouched behind a tree. From tree to tree he crept closer, until he had a full view of the camp. Two of the men were on the far side of the Stanislaus, the other three including the one in the military uniform were on this side.

Joaquín looked at the gun in his hand. He'd never fired a gun but if he could get closer, if he could push the gun at them and pull the trigger, it should work. He might get one, or two of them, maybe the three on this side, before they killed him.

He slipped from behind the tree and ran to the wagon, crouching behind it. He'd have to shoot them one at a time. How?

Suddenly one of them came out of the water toward the campfire. It was Harvey. He poured a cup of coffee and stood there drinking it, his back to the wagon.

Joaquín darted from behind the wagon, pushed the gun into the *Americano's* back, and squeezed the trigger.

No shot. No noise. Nothing. The trigger would not move.

Harvey whirled, flinging his coffee cup away, and grabbed the pistol.

Joaquín squeezed the trigger again and again. Nothing.

They struggled mightily, both holding the gun, until Harvey hooked one of Joaquín's legs with his foot and pulled Joaquín to the ground. The gun flew out of his hand and Harvey jumped back.

"Hey, it's the greaser kid!" he cried in alarm.

Sam Roberts and Bull Dutton came splashing from the river.

"Didn't I tell you to shoot that bastard on sight!" Roberts yelled.

"I ain't got my gun."

"You shoulda had your gun! Didn't I tell you to keep armed?"

Harvey sat down on a bench at the table, shaken by the surprise and closeness of his brush with death. "He had the gun in my back," he said, bewildered. "Why didn't he shoot me?"

Bull Dutton had picked up Joaquín's revolver. "It ain't even cocked," he said. "It's loaded, but it ain't cocked."

Joaquín was sitting up, shaking his head to clear it. He'd failed as he knew he would. Let them kill him. It would be better this way.

"I told you men to be on guard. I told you to wear your guns," Roberts was saying. "Look at you . . . none of you have your guns on." He pulled his own gun from its holster. "I'll kill that greaser bastard! Get out of my way!"

Before he could cock and aim his weapon, the horse came from behind the circus wagon and nuzzled Joaquín, pushing its muzzle at Joaquín's back.

"Look, he brought a horse!" said Bull.

"Where'd that horse come from?" Roberts wanted to know.

"He musta rode it in," said Bull.

"Where would he get a horse . . . a damn greaser?"

"He musta stole it!"

The other two had come from across the river by now to see what the commotion was all about.

John Little came up, tugging at his sidearm. "Let me shoot that son of a bitch. I don't want him running around loose. Not after what we done."

Roberts put a hand out to stop John Little. "Wait!"

"What for?"

"Because I'm thinking," said Roberts.

"Where's his woman?" Bull Dutton asked. "We could kill him and keep her here to cook for us."

"Yeah, for cookin' and fuckin'," added John Little.

"She might be out there in the bushes right now," said Christian, "with a rifle on us."

That alerted them. They looked around, scanning the edge of the forest.

Sam Roberts took command. "Pick him up and sit him down there," he said, pointing to a bench at the table.

And when Joaquín was on the bench, Roberts asked, "Why did you come back here?"

Joaquín looked up at this terrible *Americano* with cold hatred. "To kill you!", he spat out.

"And what else?"

Joaquín looked away. He had come back here to die, really; to avenge Rosita or to die trying. He said, "To get our things."

"Where's your woman?"

Joaquín did not answer.

"Where'd you steal that horse?"

No answer.

"Where'd you get that gun?"

No answer.

Sam Roberts put his pistol in his left hand and slapped Joaquín hard on the face. "Answer me! Damn you!"

Joaquín let his head roll and glanced up at this hated *gringo* with blazing, helpless fury.

"All right!" Roberts yelled. "He wants his things. Get him his things. Get that trunk outa the wagon."

One of the men brought the trunk. Roberts pointed for him to dump it and he did, scattering the contents in the mud and shale of the beach.

Their circus costumes. Rosita's bolero jackets, bright with metallic braid and brass buttons. He reached to pick them out of the mud and a gun cracked. Mud splattered in his face and the men howled with glee. He glanced up at them. Another bullet hit the ground beside his hand, scattering shale and bits of rock. He stood and lunged at Roberts as more bullets hit around his feet.

Roberts jammed his gun into Joaquín's belly, but that did not stop him. Joaquín clawed for the hated *Americano's* throat. Let them kill him. In his madness, Joaquín wanted only to tear out the *gringo's* eyes, choke him to death.

Roberts did not shoot. The men pulled Joaquín back and held him, powerless to move.

"Get a rope," ordered Roberts. "He's a hoss thief. And we hang hoss thieves out here."

"Attaboy, Capt'n," cried John Little. He came back

in a moment, tying a hangman's noose. The excited men put it over Joaquín's head, yanked it snug, and they dragged him to a tree at the edge of the camp.

Up over a low limb, and John Little pulled down on the other end of the rope, lifting Joaquín to tiptoes. Joaquín felt the rope burn his throat, the knot press against his ear. He gagged as his breath was cut off.

"Let up!" Roberts yelled.

John Little eased back the rope until Joaquín's heels touched ground. He stood there, trembling with fury, wobbly, gasping, supported from falling by the pull of the rope.

"We're giving you a fair trial," Roberts pronounced. "You are accused of stealing that hoss." He looked around at the group of former Regulators. "What do you say, men. Is this a hoss thief, or not? What's the verdict?"

"Yeah! Yeah!" The men slapped each other, laughing and yelling in high spirits. "Guilty!" they cried. "Hang the dirty greaser!"

"Then string him up!" ordered Sam Roberts.

John Little yanked down on his end of the rope. Joaquín gulped and choked. To die to avenge Rosita was one thing. This was another. He tried to yell. He clutched at the rope above the knot and got out a few words.

"Let him down!" Roberts yelled. "Don't you men even know how to hang somebody? You gotta tie his hands! Bull, tie that bastard's hands!"

"No!" gasped Joaquín. "You can have the horse. I did not steal it. It is my brother's."

Sam Roberts put a hand up to stop Bull. Eyes wide, mouth open, in a look of victory, he said, "You mean

65

there's another greaser claim around here?"

Joaquín sank to his knees. He had failed again. These terrible *Americanos* had gotten the best of him one more time. He'd revealed what should not have been revealed. And he was still alive. How many more would he betray if they did not kill him? Oh, why didn't they just shoot him dead?

"Turn him loose," said Roberts. "Bring him out here."

Seated on the bench again, Roberts questioned him: "Where is this camp of your brother? How many are there? Is your wife there? How far away? Which direction?"

Joaquín would not answer. He sat there, overwhelmed with feelings of shame and frustration and defeat. But not another word would he speak. He couldn't trust himself. Let them cut his tongue out. Let them torture him. Not one more word.

The draft horse he had ridden in on was still standing by. It had gone over to stand with the two circus wagon horses which had been here when the group of Regulators seized the camp.

Sam Roberts stood, thinking. The men quieted, waiting to see what their captain would do next.

Suddenly, Roberts snapped his fingers. "That hoss will lead us to their camp. Just tie the kid's hands. Sit him on the hoss and start it back upstream. All we gotta do is follow it."

The men started talking all at once. That was their captain; smart as the devil. They slapped Roberts fondly and hooted with glee. Another greaser claim meant more gold, more food and liquor and, maybe, if the woman was there, more fuckin'.

Chapter 6

"Halt!"

It was the voice of one of the cousins. He was hidden behind the trunk of a tree. Only his forehead and eyes were visible behind the rifle that extended from a fork in the tree.

When they had awakened to find Joaquín and the one horse missing, Jésus had decided to post a guard. It had been a good decision. The cousin had been able to watch the procession as it drew nearer. Joaquín, bound hand and foot, was astride the horse. Behind him trailed the *Americanos*; the first one in a military uniform, then, at irregular intervals, the others.

The cousin waited until Joaquín had passed the forked tree and it appeared that all of the *Americanos* were in view and within easy rifle range, before shouting his order to halt.

He fired a shot at the ground in front of the one in Army uniform. That shot was to alert Jésus and the other cousin, and to warn the *Americano* strangers that their lives were at stake. He stayed behind the tree as he called, "Throw down your guns."

Roberts, accepting the disadvantage of their position, carefully took his sidearm from the holster and tossed it on the ground, signaling the others to do the same.

When all guns were on the ground, the cousin stepped from behind the tree and came a few steps closer. Pointing to Joaquín, he said to Roberts, "Untie that man."

Then, when Joaquín had been untied and dismounted, he said, "Joaquín, get their guns."

At the camp, the rifle shot caused Jésus and the other cousin to drop their gold-mining tools and race toward the cabin. Inside, Rosita was asleep. As Jésus awakened her, the cousin rolled a portion of the bottom log of the back wall into the room. It made an opening into a small cell, dug back into the hill against which the cabin sat. In this secret hiding place they stored their daily accumulation of gold. A partly filled bucket of gold dust and chispa was kept in the wagon, in the event that if raiders came, they would find that bucket and look no farther.

Now Jésus hurried a sleepy Rosita into the opening.

"Down. Down," he said as he pushed her flat on the earthen floor, then into the opening.

He thrust in a blanket and rolled the log back in place.

"You stay in there," he said to the empty wall. "Make no sound. Do not move until one of us comes to let you out."

The rifle shot also alerted Bull Dutton, who had stopped to have a bowel movement and gotten so far behind the others he wasn't even trying to catch up.

Now he knew how far ahead they were and he moved

into the woods, to parallel the trail, until he could get sight of his partners and see what was up. He came upon them as the greaser kid was gathering the guns. With all attention focused on the kid picking up the guns, it was easy for Bull to slip up behind the greaser with the rifle and put a gun in his back.

"You want me to put a bullet in him, Capt'n?" Bull Dutton called out as he jammed his sixgun hard in the cousin's back and reached around to knock the rifle up and take it away.

John Little dove at Joaquín and knocked him to the ground, scattering the guns.

"Yeah, shoot the bastard." Sam Roberts breathed a sigh of relief as he lowered his arms.

Bull Dutton squeezed the trigger. The cousin jerked upward, twisted, and fell.

"That greasy bastard had us cold," Roberts was saying. "Gotta be more careful, you can't trust these greasers." Then, "Get your guns, men. Tie that damn kid up again. Spread out. Their claim must be right up ahead. We're close."

The Regulators came to the edge of the woods as Jésus and the other cousin came splashing across the creek which fed into the Stanislaus. Only a few shots dropped them. Jésus and the cousin didn't even get a chance to shoot back, because they never saw anything to shoot at.

Seated at the table in the middle of the campsite, finishing off the pot of stew they found cooking over the fire, the four former Regulators and their captain discussed their new conquest.

"This ain't as good a claim as the one we had," said

Sam Roberts. "All we found is that half a bucket of dust."

"Yeah, but we got a lot of good food," said Bull Dutton, as he stuffed a spoonful of the hot stew into his mouth, "and some tools and blankets, and them horses, and this liquor." He took a swallow from a bottle and passed it on.

"And we got rid of some more greasers," said Christian.

"I vote we go back," said Roberts. "Throw all this stuff in the wagon and let the horses pull it back to our old claim."

"That's all right with me, Capt'n," said Christian.

"I wonder where that woman is," John Little wondered.

"What do you say, Harvey?" Roberts asked.

"Whatever *you* say, Capt'n."

"And you, Bull? You wantta go back?"

"Sure, Capt'n, but let's finish up this liquor first."

"So be it!" Roberts stood up. "But we gotta leave a sign for any other greasers who come around here." He paced back and forth a moment, thinking. Then said, "I got it! Christ, go get those two we shot in the crick."

While Christian went to drag Jésus and the cousin out of the creek where they still lay, Roberts said, "John, make up some nooses. We're gonna leave these spics hangin' here for a warning."

"I wonder where that woman got to." John Little was still wondering, but he went to get some rope. "How many you want, Capt'n?"

"Just three. We're gonna have some fun with that damn kid. Teach him a lesson. Harvey, go get that kid, and that other one back on the trail."

Christian had dragged the two out of the water. He dropped them beside the table. "Hey, Capt'n, this one's still kicking."

Jésus was still alive, laboring to speak halting words in Spanish. Roberts, who was selecting a hanging tree, and had chosen one over by the corral, looked down at the two wet bodies. He said, "Shut him the hell up."

Then he said, "No! Don't shoot him. We're gonna hang him. Just shut him up."

Christian shrugged, put his gun back, and kicked Jésus in the face with his heavy miner's boot.

"Bring 'em over here," Roberts ordered, walking to the hanging tree he'd selected. "John, get those nooses on and string 'em up."

Waiting for Harvey to come back, they loaded everything worth taking into the wagon and hitched up the two horses. Roberts took the wagon whip, shortened it, and tied several knots in the end of the plaited leather. He tried it, giving the trunk of the tree a few loud whacks, and was satisfied.

When Harvey came in, dragging the dead cousin, with Joaquín walking in front, the former Regulators were all at the table, finishing the last of the liquor.

Sam Roberts stood and took command. "Get that dead one strung up, John. Christian, strip that damn kid and tie him to the tree." He shook out the wagon whip and made it crack like a rifle shot. "We're gonna whip that one to death."

The men glanced at each other. They hadn't expected this new twist. The whole raid had been a disappointment; no real action, they hadn't found as much gold or liquor as they hoped for, and no sign of the woman. But now, thanks to their captain, they were at least going to have some fun.

They pounced on Joaquín, talking excitedly, yanked off his clothes and bound him to the trunk of the hanging tree. Joaquín did not try to fight them. After seeing the bodies of Jésus and the two cousins, he wanted only to die, also. The sooner, the better.

As the men stepped back after tying him, Joaquín thought about Rosita. Where was she? How was she? To think of his wife, his little dove, brought shame and he could only be thankful she was not here to see the indignity of his dying. But where could she be?

Roberts was standing apart, still cracking the whip. The men were waiting for the fun to begin. Roberts let the whip drag on the ground. He turned to look back at the table.

"Bull!" he yelled. "Get your ass up, away from that food, and come over here. You get first crack at him."

Rosita Felix Carillo had little hope for the future. True, she was alive. She had survived one ordeal and now lay hidden from the terrible *Americanos* who were, at this very moment, despoiling the camp of her brother-in-law and two cousins. But what had happened to these, her people, her family? Had they fled? Had they been killed? Where was Joaquín? What had happened to him? When would they come to rescue her?

From within the dark cell, lying prone on the blanket Jésus had stuffed inside at the last moment, she had heard the brief flurry of gunshots. Then heard the voices of the terrible *Americanos* as they came closer, talking in their loud, harsh, excited accents. She heard

72

them come into the cabin, search it, and go outside to continue their plunder.

For the moment she was safe. They had not discovered the sawn log in the back wall of the cabin. And while they had been in the cabin, Rosita had held her breath, fearing they might hear the sound of her breathing.

Now their voices were distant. Occasionally, she could hear the one who wore the military uniform, the Captain Roberts, giving orders. She would never forget his voice or his face, from that first desecration of their lives and property. She would never forget any of them: The gluttonous one they called Bull; John Little, the tall one who had first violated her; Harvey, whom she had liked and trusted; and the deadly, quiet one named Christian.

As long as she lived, if she lived, she would never forget the horror of that night, nor forget the men whom she and Joaquín had welcomed as neighbors, in good faith and trust.

Outside, she heard cracking sounds that sounded like gunshots, and yet did not sound exactly like gunshots. Then more of these cracking sounds, accompanied by excited whoops and howling laughter.

Finally, she heard, ''Gitap! Gitap!'' the harsh shouts of a *gringo* driving horses. Then the creaking of wagon wheels moving away. Then nothing but silence.

She lay there a long while listening, wondering if they would come back. She wondered if one of them was still there, if any of her own people were still around, if Joaquín was still alive and if he would come for her.

After what seemed like hours, with no sound of any

kind beyond the log wall of the cabin, she ventured to push at the log which sealed the entrance. It would not move.

A feeling of terror seized her. She could not sit up; the roof of this secret cell was not more than a foot above her head as she lay prone, staring at blackness. She reached out to feel the back wall with one hand. She had to get out. Her body demanded that she get out or she would befoul herself. She moved to brace her body against the back wall and pushed at the log with both hands. It would not move.

The sensation of terror increased. She was getting desperate, frantic. If the *Americanos* were out there or not, she had to escape this living grave. To be killed by them would be better than to be buried alive. She pressed her back against the rear wall of the cell and drew her knees up to her chest, and kicked out with both feet at the log.

It budged, thank God.

She reached down with her hand to place her feet in the right spot on the log and pressed, and prayed, and pushed. With her back against the rear wall, she pushed with both feet, with all her might.

The log moved ever so slightly. Then rolled away.

Rosita collapsed. Light was coming through the opening from the open doorway of the cabin. She breathed deep in relief and felt her whole body relax, the terror recede.

Then alert, she listened. Still no sound from outside.

She had to go. It felt as if her belly would burst. She wriggled to the opening, looked out, saw nothing but the disarray of the cabin, as the raiders had left it. She wormed her body out through the narrow opening, then lay a moment on the floor of the cabin, listening.

There was no sound. She stood, supporting herself against the back wall of the cabin. Still no sounds. The daylight that came through the cabin door was not bright. It must be twilight. In the dim light, she stepped over the log and moved to the doorway. Staying inside the doorframe, she looked out.

In the twilight, the camp and the woods beyond lay peaceful and quiet. The fire was a bright spot of glowing orange coals in the deepening shadows. The river reflected a pinkish light from the sky. There was no sign of movement, no sound, save the bird calls in the wood.

She stepped outside and turned to go behind the wagon to relieve herself and saw that it was gone. The *Americanos* had stolen it. That was the sound of wagon wheels rolling away she had heard. Her eyes swept to the empty corral, horses gone, gate open. Then, beyond the fencing of the corral, she saw the bodies hanging from the tree.

"Madre de Dios!"

The strength drained from her. She sank to her knees and felt warm urine flow.

With both hands she covered her eyes to blot out the sight. *"Oh, my God! My God!"* she mumbled. *"Those terrible Americanos! They have massacred my people!"* She felt a wave of faintness sweep over her. She steeled herself, forced herself to look, to stand, and walk closer. Saw that it was Jésus and the two cousins hanging. Then saw Joaquín tied to the tree trunk. His naked and bleeding body sagged limp and lifeless against the ropes that bound him.

Rosita collapsed again. This time, mercifully, she fainted.

When she regained consciousness it was dark, but moonlight revealed the tree's bitter fruit and the limp body bound to the trunk. The horror of the sight revived her—she beat the ground with both fists in wild uncontrollable fury. No tears. Just rage. A poisonous hatred was growing in her heart.

All dead; she couldn't conceive it. Her whole world gone. Her Joaquín, so gentle, so kind, his naked body striped with lash marks dripping blood. This was a greater desecration than the violation of her own body by these terrible *Americanos*.

If only I could die now, also, she thought, for her grief was unbearable. With both hands she tore at her hair, trying to pull it out by the roots; this thing her man had loved so much. She tore at her shirt in a madness of agony, ripped it apart, and beat her breasts, wailing an animal cry of grief. With fingernails, she clawed her cheeks, her breasts, her belly, to give pain and punishment to this wretched body that lived on when the heart of her had died with the man she loved.

Suddenly, she stopped. She banged her head with clenched fists to stop the wild whirling of her mind. She looked away from the tree trunk with its sagging lump of human flesh, remembering. Like a vision of the past before dying, she recalled all the years of her love for Joaquín, from the time she was a child.

Then, to comfort herself, she relived the short span of their marriage. The time could be counted in days, so brief a span. She remembered each time of lovemaking, each and every meal they had shared, recalled each time they had performed together, the galloping, golden horses, the costumes, the applauding crowds. And she thought of the sons they never had, the home they had never built, the holidays they would never be able to celebrate together.

A chill swept through her. She stood and moved to the fire. She placed wood on the still-glowing coals and squatted on her heels, staring at the growing flame.

Rosita Felix Carillo had fainted dead away and died in that moment. Rosita Carillo, wife of Joaquín Carillo, had been a woman full of love and tenderness, bursting with the joy of living, overflowing with kindness and mercy and good faith and trust in all humanity.

This was a new woman who now crouched at the fire; a woman filled with hatred, a woman lusting for vengeance, a woman with only one purpose: to kill the terrible *Americanos*.

How? When? The woman did not know. But the soul within her would find a way. The cold heart would keep beating, driving her, until she feasted on the sight of those terrible *Americanos* dying in their own blood.

Like the apostles of Christ, she gave herself a new name for the new woman in this transformed body.

Antonia Molinera.

Where she dredged that name from out of her subconscious mind, she never knew. Was it the name of some distant ancestor who had died in the Spanish Inquisition, dying to protect her family? Was it a wife who crossed the wide uncharted ocean with one of the family forebearers, facing fearlessly into the unknown, standing strong beside a man who searched for a new world of freedom?

Wherever it came from, she was now Antonia Molinera, and would so be until she washed her hands in the blood of these terrible *Americanos*. Her vow was made. This night would be her vigil.

She piled more wood on the fire and glanced back at the scene of horror, to implant it in her mind, never to be forgotten.

The dancing flames cast an apparition. Joaquín had moved in his bonds. She darted across to the tree and tore at the knots. Finally, her fingers bleeding, the nails torn off, Joaquín slumped to the ground.

She bent over him, touching his face, calling his name.

"Madre de Dios!" He stirred, his lips moved in a murmur.

She stood, her mind whirling. Then she raced to the cabin and dragged a pallet to the body. She rolled his limp form onto the pallet, then dragged him to the fire.

She got water from the stream, tore the other pallet cover into strips, and bathed the blood from his face and body. She lifted his head to make him drink.

When he began to shake with a chill, she uttered cries of praise unto God, rejoicing that he was truly alive, or that the dead had come back to life. Then she lay beside him, holding his body to hers, and covered them with the other pallet. Praying, she held him tight. Joaquín, her Joaquín. Her body would warm him. Her breath would keep him breathing. Her spirit would not let him die.

Her night of vigil became a night of unceasing prayer.

Chapter 7

It was two days later before Joaquín was strong enough to go outside the cabin. The new Rosita—Antonia Molinera—had caught fish in the river to feed him and kept the fire going to cook the fish. She washed his clothes and dressed him and kept his wounds clean. Also, she found a pickaxe and shovel the raiders had left behind, and had dug three graves.

Now, as she helped Joaquín outside and led him to the three holes she'd dug, condors flew up from the branches of the hanging tree. They looked up, saw that the eyes had been pecked out, and flesh torn from the faces and the bodies.

Joaquín reeled. He staggered back to a bench at the table and sat down. He supported his head in both hands, covering his eyes to squeeze out that gruesome sight.

Antonia stood beside him. "They must be buried," she said.

Joaquín lifted his head and nodded numb agreement.

"They are too heavy for me to get down."

Joaquín nodded again, dumbly. He kept his eyes fixed upon some distant spot across the sparkling water of the river so he would not see the tree's horrid burden.

She sat on the bench beside him. "Joaquín, look at me."

He turned slowly, saw the scratches on her face, unhealed yet, saw her torn and disheveled clothing, her tangled hair, and to hide the tears that came welling in his eyes, he clutched her to him and buried his face in that tangled hair.

She pushed him away and stood up.

"Joaquín!" She spoke sharply.

He looked up at her, blinking away the tears.

"Rosita?" he asked softly.

"Agh!" She expelled her breath harshly and turned from his sorrowful, puzzled, questioning eyes. She walked a few steps away, then back, steeling herself, rejecting all tenderness, fighting down compassion. This was no time for love or understanding. She was a new woman with only hatred, only vengeance, in her heart. It had to begin here and now.

She stood with hands on hips. "Do not call me by that name! I am no more Rosita!" she stated emphatically.

Then, because she could not stand the puzzled look in his eyes, his bewildered expression, she took both his hands in hers and knelt before him.

"Joaquín, I took a vow," she explained. "No more am I Rosita. No more am I your woman and your wife. Until these terrible *Americanos* who did this thing are dead, I am Antonia Molinera. Until that Captain Roberts is dead in his own blood, I cannot think of anything else. I cannot be anything else but Antonia Molinera, a woman of vengeance."

Joaquín pulled away from her. He stood and backed

away. The whole world was insane. Something had happened to Rosita, or something was wrong in his own brain. As Rosita arose and came toward him, he backed up to the graves and was caught between two terrors.

"Joaquín, you must come with me. You must help me. Together we will kill this Captain Roberts." She caught his hand. "You must make a vow, too. Say it! You will kill these terrible *Americanos*."

"Rosita . . ." He waved his free hand helplessly. "I don't know how." His eyes pled with her. "I tried once to kill them. That is why I went back. And it's because of that, that this has happened. Jésus, my brother, was right. We cannot fight them."

Rosita threw his hand from hers. Cold, flashing anger was in her eyes now, a deadly determination in her expression. She rose on tiptoes and spat full in his face.

Joaquín recoiled. With one hand he touched the spittle on his face. He couldn't believe what was happening.

Rosita—Antonia—flung one hand up in a sharp gesture of dismissal that pointed to the hanging tree.

"Bury those bodies!" she snarled at him. "Then bury yourself, too! Because you are dead to me! No more do I have a man. Antonia Molinera has no one. She is alone!" She swept both hands downward in a sharp and final gesture.

Her eyes burned into his as she continued speaking, now softly, vehemently, "I will have to kill this Captain Roberts myself. Antonia Molinera will do it alone." She raised clenched fists and shook them in Joaquín's face. "With these—my own two hands—I will avenge my honor!"

81

She turned abruptly from his startled, dumbfounded expression, as if she could no longer stand the sight of him, and started for the cabin.

Joaquín could find no words to answer her. There was no way to understand or express his amazement. He stood there, physically shocked for the moment. Rosita—this new Antonia—was a total stranger to him. The whole sequence of horror upon horror of these last days was too overwhelming to absorb. There had not yet been time enough for his mind to sort it out and respond.

He looked around uncertainly, and then tensed when his eyes caught the hanging bodies. They must be buried. His scrambled brain registered that thought. Here, at least, was a simple, acceptable task that had to be done. Something he could do. Something that made sense.

Dumbly, he moved to the tree and busied himself lowering the bodies.

Two mounds in a row, two graves filled gently with untamped earth, because of the bodies lying below. And one more empty hole to fill. Joaquín laid his shovel aside and went to get the body of his brother, Jésus. He knelt to pick him up. He put one arm under Jésus' shoulders and saw the mutilated face, the empty eyesockets, the torn flesh, and burst into tears.

"Oh, brother of my youth . . ." he sobbed and pressed the bloody head to his bosom. Jésus had first taught him to ride. It was Jésus who gave him his love of the horses, who was his constant companion and protector, who had worked side by side with him in their father's vineyards, ridden with him on the trail, slept beside him under the stars.

"You said that you would die for me," he was talking to the corpse but, at that moment, the dead brother in his arms seemed to be more of reality than this unreal world which had suddenly engulfed him. "Oh, God, I never meant it to end this way," he pledged to the cold body in his arms. "I never thought this evil of these terrible *Americanos* would touch you, my brother."

Joaquín raised his head and saw, through a blurry mist of tears, the cabin where Rosita had disappeared. His thoughts were clear and understandable now. Rosita was right. These terrible *Americanos* must pay for this carnage with their lives.

He raised his face to the heavens. "Oh, Jésus, my brother," he cried, and now he was talking to God, or to his brother's soul which had departed. "Now I will die for you," he sobbed.

He lifted the limp form and laid it gently in the grave. Blinded by tears, he filled the hole. Three mounds in a row.

As he stood there looking at them, a flash of movement caught his eye and he glanced up to see Rosita leaving the cabin. She had a sack, made of the pallet cover, over one shoulder and, in her other hand, she carried the pickaxe. She had stuffed the bottoms of her pants into a pair of men's boots. Her long black hair had been hacked off short so that from this distance she looked like a boy.

Joaquín threw aside the shovel and raced toward her.

"Rosita!"

She didn't stop, just kept walking away without even looking at him.

"Rosita!" He was behind her and he caught her arm and pulled her around to face him. "Your hair—" he cried. "What did you do to your hair?"

She yanked her arm free and raized the pickaxe to strike him. He caught the tool and tore it from her grasp. She stood glaring at him, panting in her anger.

"I am no more Rosita! I am *Antonia*!"

"Where are you going?"

"That is none of your affair!"

"Tell me!" He grabbed her shoulders and shook her. "What are you going to do?"

"What I must do! Kill this Captain Roberts!"

"No! You will not!" he shouted.

She tried to pull away. Joaquín held her.

"He must die!" she cried. "All of them!"

Joaquín took her by the arm. He dragged her to the three mounds.

Pointing down at the three graves, he stated softly, "I will avenge these: my brother, my cousins. It is I who will kill this Captain Roberts."

Tears were pouring from his eyes as he stared down at the newly mounded earth, and murmured, "For these so dear to me"—then his head lifted and he moved one arm in a wide sweeping gesture that took in all of the surrounding hills—"and for all of my countrymen, too!"

Rosita dropped her sack and clutched at him. The strength which had sustained her through these last days drained away and she sank to the ground, pulling Joaquín to his knees as he embraced her. Kneeling there, clutching each other, he touched her shorn hair and tears flowed again at the sight of it. She tenderly touched the bruises and whip marks on his face.

Suddenly, she caught his shoulders, saying, "Then you can no longer be the kind and gentle man I loved. From now on, you will be Murrieta! Killer! Avenger!"

He nodded agreement, blinking away the tears. Whatever she wanted, he would do, because the violation she had suffered was a dishonor that could never be requited, a degradation that no retribution could ever undo.

He released her, this woman who was a stranger to him, but still his Rosita, his little dove of yesterday, and lifted his hands and looked at them, wondering how these hands could ever accomplish what he must do. Still nodding, he bit out the words, "Until these hands of mine are dyed deep in the blood of this Captain Roberts."

He stood abruptly. Rosita's hands caught at his belt, holding on, as she looked up at him. From where she knelt, he looked enormous as he raised clenched fists above his head. Shaking his fists at the heavens, he shouted to the surrounding hills, *"Yo soy Joaquín!"* I am Joaquín.

Again his cry broke the forest stillness.

"Joaquín Murrieta!"

PART II

Chapter 8

In the summer of 1849, Clark's Point in San Francisco, which had been named for an elder of the Mormon church, was the center of sin and corruption that sustained the men working the gold fields. The one main street offered nothing but saloons and gambling establishments. There were few permanent buildings. Most of the attractions were housed in tents, with a bar made up of a plank set across two whiskey barrels and the rest of the area rented out to dealers in games of faro, three-card monte, the shell game, and poker.

Behind this one main street, brightly lighted at night with torches and kerosene lights, was a colony of Spanish-speaking and Chinese harlots. The girls lived and worked in canvas tents, packing-box shanties, and adobe mud huts. The Mexican and South American whores were mainly independents, women from sixteen to thirty-five, who solicited their own business and set their own prices. On the other hand, the Chinese were all fed, clothed, and housed by masters, or managers, who imported girls, ten to twelve years of age. They were children of peasant families in the Orient who would sell a child to a procurer for a bag of rice. All of the harlots had the French disease. Few of the Chinese children lived through their adolescence.

On the night of July 10, 1849, Samuel Roberts and his gang of Regulators marched into this area of disease and degeneracy. Back from the gold fields to spend their gain in San Francisco, Roberts organized and led the attack with military dispatch.

In the darkness, the Regulators surrounded the colony of harlots. Then, at a given signal, they moved in from all sides, raping the women and clubbing their customers, shooting when necessary, tearing down the flimsy shelters, and carrying off what meager possessions they could find.

In one tent, Juan Garcia, a Mexican, about twenty-eight years old, had removed his gunbelt and hat and was kneeling beside a Chinese girl of about thirteen years of age, who was lying on her back on a grass mat. Juan had removed her quilted pantaloons, and pushed up the smocklike top she wore, to discover the exotic beauty, and direction, of this lotus blossom.

In the soft light of a kerosene lantern hanging from the tent pole, the child seemed unreal, not human flesh. Her extreme youth, the beauty of her flawless ivory skin, the delicate dolllike features and slanting eyes, the tender brown nipples of breasts just beginning to swell in her puberty, aroused him in a strangely unnatural way. The child had only a beginning fuzz of pubic hair, the folds of her vagina were smooth and unwrinkled.

He passed one hand over the poreless porcelain flesh of thigh and hip and her body trembled. Juan sighed as he felt a warm stream of blood flood his groin.

Outside, the Chinese master who was keeping watch over five of his tents, saw the Regulators close in, heard the sounds of terror and violence come closer, and disappeared into the night without giving any warning.

Inside, Juan Garcia was prolonging this strange, delightful feeling. His hand gently caressed other parts of the child's flawless, immature body. He smiled and nodded when the girl smiled up at him because he was being gentle. The warm flush of passion in his groin had his flesh swollen and throbbing with an exquisite ache.

Suddenly, the tent was ripped away, the lantern kicked aside, and he became aware of the activity and sounds in the darkness surrounding him. Burning shanties and tents cast a flickering illumination on the scene of destruction and violence. It revealed two of the Regulators standing over him. One held a hatchet. The other had a lantern in one hand and a pickaxe handle in the other.

His gunbelt was beyond reach. Juan Garcia rolled aside, trying to get to his feet, and pulled a knife out of his left boot. Too slow. The man with the lantern stomped on his wrist. The other chopped at his hand with the hatchet, cutting off the last two fingers.

Juan did not feel the pain because, at the same moment, the one with the lantern hit him with the pickaxe handle. Groggy, he saw the *Americano* who had cut off his fingers grab the child, who was screaming hysterically and trying to get away. He saw him throw her to the mat and fall atop her, holding her with one hand while with the other he worked to get his fly open.

Another blow of the pickaxe handle ended the scene.

Nearby, in a shanty made of the wood of packing crates, William Burns, the gambler, was about to reach climax when he was yanked off and out of the Mexican harlot with whom he was cohabiting. Strong hands held him in a bearlike grip while he struggled to pull up his trousers to cover his erection.

The two Regulators who had broken into the shanty howled with laughter as they watched his ineffective attempts to cover himself. Then they took turns, one raping the woman, while the other held Burns helpless. After the rapes, one of them calmly pointed a pistol at the gambler.

"Your money."

"Sure. Sure." Burns pulled his pants up at last and offered them a pocketful of gold coins.

The other Regulator grabbed him by his coat lapels. "All of it!" he roared.

"Sure. Sure." Burns reached into an inside pocket and brought out a billfold.

The Regulator grabbed it and slammed Burns against the wall of the shanty. "Now you get with us and help clear out this bunch of furriners. Yuh hear me."

"Sure."

"You start by burning this shack down." He handed Burns the oil lamp.

"Sure. But what about her?" Burns pointed to the woman who had crawled into a corner, cowering in fright.

"Just start burning. If she can't crawl out, let her burn up, too."

The gambler nodded. The men moved back to the canvas-covered entrance, one of them still holding the gun on him. Burns poured the kerosene from the well of the lamp onto the floor. Looking back, he saw the men were still watching him, and he took the chimney off the lamp and dropped the burning wick into the pool of kerosene.

As flames reached out in all directions, he looked back again. The Regulators were gone. He darted to the woman, grabbed up her clothes, and helped her past the spreading flames, out through the doorway, and to a safe distance. There he helped her dress as they watched the burning shanty illuminate the scenes of havoc all around them.

Later, as dawn was lighting the eastern sky, Joaquín (now Murrieta) and Antonia Molinera (Rosita) rode in upon this scene of desolation and despair. The sight of blood, of dead and wounded, turned Joaquín's stomach and he glanced around at his young wife. In that glance was all the revulsion and uncertainty he felt, all the rebellion of his gentle nature against any and all acts of violence and brutality, to which he was now committed.

Antonia read the complex meanings of that glance. She knew her man, his soft heart and peaceful ways. Those were the very characteristics she had fallen in love with when first she gave her heart and soul to him in childhood devotion. Her heart ached for him, but she was no more that young Rosita, that happy girl so much in love. Antonia Molinera was a woman sworn to vengeance.

She steeled herself. She gave him a cold, hard look of contempt and spat on the ground between their horses. Then spurred her horse forward through the still-smouldering ruins.

''My people!'' she called in a loud voice. Again,

"My people!" She waved both hands to draw them to her.

Joaquín reined his horse up beside her and they sat side by side, as the bewildered and wretched survivors of the night's carnage stirred themselves and slowly moved closer.

As the crowd gathered, looking up at these two strangers with vacant expressions of defeat and despair, Joaquín stood in his stirrups. He raised one hand.

"Yo soy Joaquín!"

The crowd was unmoved. They stared up at him with vacant, beaten mien. No one spoke.

"I am Joaquín Murrieta!" cried Joaquín. "I will avenge this act of these terrible *Americanos*! This is *our* land . . . *our* country . . . yours and mine. It is *our* gold that they steal from us!"

There was a stirring in the crowd. The women and the few men looked around at each other. Murmurings were heard: the word, "Murrieta?" Another word, "Avenger?"

"This is Antonia Molinera, my woman," Joaquín continued. "She has been violated by these same spoilers who have done this to you." He yanked off his shirt and stood tall in the saddle, there in the early morning light, so they could see the stripes and whip lashes which marred his body.

"They have beaten me to death, but I have lived. They have killed my brother, and my cousins. They have stolen our gold. They steal your gold. They rape our women. They kill us. They would drive us from this land which is rightfully ours."

The crowd was coming alive now, cursing the terrible *Americanos*. Like filings drawn to a magnet, they were now charged with purpose, with a new direction, because there was a leader.

Joaquín sat in his saddle. He let them talk among themselves for a moment. Then he said, "I need your help. Will you come back into the hills with me to make an army, to fight these terrible *Americanos* who will destroy us if we do not stand together?"

The crowd wavered. They asked each other who could fight these terrible *Americanos*. The few men tried to disappear. They had only come to Clark's Point last night to find a woman; one moment of fleeting joy, not a cause to die for.

Antonia called out, "Who will join us?"

One of the harlots answered, "I will!" and moved through the crowd toward Antonia.

Joaquín stood in his stirrups again. He threw one hand toward the heavens, splashed red and gold with the rising sun, and cried in a loud voice:

"Yo soy Joaquín! Who will join Joaquín?"

One man pushed through the crowd of women. It was Juan Garcia. His left hand was wrapped with a bloody rag, and the harlots made way willingly for this angry man. When at last he stood beside Joaquín's horse, he offered his good hand to pledge his support. Joaquín's face lighted as he reached down to clasp it.

"Un hombre bueno!" he cried and yanked Juan Garcia up behind him on the horse.

Then to the crowd: "Who else will ride with Murrieta to avenge our countrymen?"

Only two more of the women moved forward. The others gradually turned back to their own affairs of salvaging what they could of this present wreckage. Among themselves they murmured, qualifying their passive natures. Who could fight these terrible *Americanos*? Was it not better to live, to go home one day? Was it not better to avoid a conflict that could only end in death?

Joaquín looked around at his Rosita, at Antonia, and shrugged. *"Vamos!"* he said to her and to the women who remained with her. He turned his horse and started away. Not much had been won, but he had made a first step, and there had been a light of admiration in Antonia's eyes; that was reward of a kind.

A hand caught his saddle and he reined up. It was the gambler, William Burns, looking up at him.

"I cannot kill my own people," said Burns, "but here, take this." He held out a small deadly derringer.

Joaquín shrank back, away from the gun which represented everything his gentle nature opposed. Somehow he must avenge himself and his countrymen, but guns, killing, violence . . . These things were so completely foreign to his character, so abhorrent to him, a sense of revulsion seemed to drain from his head to his toes, causing him to shiver in the heat of the day. It left him weak and empty. But if not by killing and violence, how then?

Antonia ended his indecision. She rode up beside him. She reached across his saddle and took the weapon.

The gambler, looking poised and dapper in his striped pants, brocade vest and broadcloth coat, so proper amid all this confusion and bloody disarray, lifted one soft white hand to remove his high hat and bow slightly.

"William Burns, ma'am," he said. "If ever I can be of help, I will."

• • •

The road out of Stockton was the main access to the southern gold fields. Before reaching the foothills of the Sierra Nevada mountain range, it traveled through areas of natural parkland of tall grasses and wild oat, dotted with ancient oaks. In this primeval Eden there were grizzly bears that weighed a thousand pounds, great herds of elk, deer and antelope, and overhead the sky darkened at times with flights of geese, swan, duck, partridge, crane, and pelican.

Bands of wild horses and wild cattle ranged over the plains and golden hills. The many streams and creeks held trout and fat, lazy salmon. Within the forest glade and by these flashing waters lived otter, raccoon, beaver, squirrel, the predatory wildcat, mountain lion, and cougar. And there were Indians, decendants of original immigrant tribes that had crossed the Aleutians from Mongolia.

On this road traveled the miners going in and coming out of the southern diggings. Other traffic on the road included the many supply wagons carrying lumber and hardware, beans, flour, bacon, canned fruit, and barrels of molasses and whiskey that had sailed around the Horn.

Where this road entered a wooded area Joaquín, Antonia, and Juan Garcia, whom they now called Three-Fingered Jack, sat their horses, hidden in the trees, as a small supply train of two wagons approached. Two men sat on the driver's seat of each wagon.

As the wagons entered the cover of the woods, the three of them spurred their mounts forward.

"Yo soy Joaquín!"

97

Joaquín yelled as he rode down upon the lead horses and they reared back in fright. Three-Fingered Jack dashed past the first wagon, calmly shooting the rider on the driver's seat, then reined up beside the second wagon and shot both rider and driver.

Antonia, with her short hair, wearing a shirt and breeches stuffed into boots, looked like another man. She held the driver of the first wagon at gunpoint. He had his hands up, pleading mercy. With the gun, she motioned him down and he stood with his back to the front wheel of the wagon, his hands high, trembling in fright.

Joaquín had calmed the horses. Jack rode back to where Antonia sat her horse with the derringer pointed at the quaking driver. As Jack sighted his pistol to shoot the man, Antonia stopped him.

"No! Tie him to the wagon wheel."

They exchanged glances.

"I think it is better that we kill him," said Jack.

"No! Do as I say."

Jack shrugged and holstered his gun. He dismounted and tied one of the man's legs to a spoke of the wheel.

Joaquín had dismounted and came up to them. He looked at the three dead *Americanos* and a frown twisted his young face.

"We did it, no?" said Antonia, looking down at him from her seat in the saddle.

He glanced up. *"Sí."*

"It is easy, no?" said Antonia. "These *Americanos* die like everyone else. The same guns they use to kill our countrymen will also kill them."

"Sí." Joaquín had to agree. But he did not have to like it and his face showed his dislike. He said, "Let us

bury these dead *gringos*. Then we will take the wagons.''

Three-Fingered Jack laughed. "Ho! No, my *capitan*. We will just carry them back into the bushes. The wolves will take care of them.''

Joaquín nodded. He didn't approve, but had to agree. What did it matter to these dead if their bodies lay in an unmarked grave, or if their bones lay under a covering of leaves on the forest floor?

"Well, let's do it and get out of here.'' He reached for the body still on the wagon seat.

Antonia stopped him.

"Wait!''

Joaquín braced himself. He knew something more was coming. He looked around at her.

"There is another.'' She pointed with her gun at the man tied to the wagon wheel.

"Let him go. We got the supplies. That's what we came for.''

"Oh, no, my *capitan*,'' Three-Fingered Jack was quick to disagree. "We cannot let this one go. He saw us kill.''

Joaquín glanced from Antonia to Jack, his two partners, the only two people in this land he could trust, and had to agree. Too often now he had to agree with the disagreeable. The logic of violence was always the opposite of what his heart would have him do, what his mind told him was right. He'd have to learn a new way to think because the right thing now was what had always before been the wrong thing.

He looked at the frightened driver, cringing before him, and could not feel hatred in his heart. True, this man was one of the *Americanos*, but this one had done nothing to deserve death. This *gringo* was no killer. This man had not despoiled any of the Spanish-speaking peoples. This was not one of the terrible *Americanos* who called themselves the Regulators.

The man sank to his knees, clasping his hands in an attitude of prayer.

"Oh, please, I got a wife and kids back east."

Joaquín turned away from those pleading eyes.

"I just come west to make my fortune."

The voice pierced Joaquín's heart.

"I'm goin' home again. They're waitin' fer me."

Joaquín kicked viciously at a rock in the road. He looked up at Antonia. She was holding out a sixgun Jack had taken from one of the dead men.

"Ah, no!" Joaquín backed away from her.

She dismounted and came toward him, pushing the gun at him.

"Take it!" She offered the weapon, her eyes locked with his. "Kill him! Kill the *Americano*!"

"No—no!" Joaquín backed away from those wild eyes, away from this woman who was a stranger he did not know, and bumped into Three-Fingered Jack.

"Ah, Antonia—" said Jack. "Let him alone. Let me do it." He started to withdraw his gun.

"NO!" Her voice cracked like a whip. "He must do it himself! He must kill the *Americano*."

She crouched before Joaquín, looking up at him with blazing eyes. "Think of your brother, Jésus. Think of our cousins." Her voice was rising. "Think of yourself, how they beat you and whipped you to death." Her voice was a scream now as she yelled, "Think of *me*!"

She thrust the gun into his hand and forced him to face the wagon driver.

"*Pull it!* Squeeze the trigger!" she screamed.

Joaquín pointed the gun. He closed his eyes and contracted his fingers. The gun crashed and leaped in his hand.

The shock of it opened his eyes and he saw the wagon driver writhing in the dust of the road, scrabbling to crawl under the wagon.

"*Kill him! Shoot!*" Antonia screamed.

And when Joaquín would have opened his hand to let the gun drop, she grasped his hand, aimed the pistol, and forced his finger on the trigger to squeeze off the shots again and again. The wagon driver jerked and twitched on the ground with each shot, suffering an agony of pain, until Three-Fingered Jack mercifully put a bullet between his eyes and the body relaxed in death.

Chapter 9

The first winter in the gold fields was passed quietly in Hornitos, in Mariposa County, a settlement of Mexican and Spanish-speaking gamblers and desperados and their women, who had been driven out of other camps on the lode. Claudio rejoined them, with a few of the in-laws and cousins from Sonora, and his presence made their lives happier.

With snow twenty feet deep in the gulches, mining operations throughout the mother lode were suspended and survival became of paramount importance.

Safe in Hornitos, Joaquín and Antonia were able to reestablish some measure of their life together. It was their love which bound them, but if there was no lovemaking between them—since Antonia was not woman, nor wife, but only a spirit of vengeance—there was at least a mutual respect. There was also the memory of what their life had been before it was disrupted by the terrible *Americanos*.

The few victories of Murrieta, and his increasing number of followers, united against the *gringos*, salved some of the bitterness and helped them accept their lot. But never could they forget the horrors of the past summer.

Antonia had other women to talk to. Joaquín and Claudio, looking like twin brothers, were together constantly. Three-Fingered Jack who had, in a way, taken the place of his brother, Jésus, in Joaquín's broken heart became his chief adviser and second-in-command.

Through the long nights they argued and talked of the unjust acquisition of Alta California by the *Americanos*. They made plans to rid the land of these Yankee gold diggers and get the gold into Mexican hands, where it rightfully belonged.

Other Spanish-speaking immigrants who had been driven from their claims by the *Americanos* joined the band. By spring, there were about twenty compatriots, half of them women who, like Antonia, wore shirt, pants, and boots and could ride and shoot as well as any of the men. All were pledged to Murrieta's crusade of vengeance.

The first news of a new gold strike reached Hornitos in April 1850. It was brought back by the owner of the Fandango house when he returned from a trip to Stockton, braving muddy trails and flooded streams, to replenish his liquor supplies.

The next morning Murrieta rode.

They reached the spot on Wood's Creek the following day. Joaquín, Three-Fingered Jack, and Claudio rode into the camp to look it over while the others of the band, under Antonia, remained hidden in the forest a half mile away.

Fourteen miners were working the spot, with individual claims about ten by twenty feet, laid out side by side, on both the south and north banks of the creek. As usual, the miners greeted the strangers with tales of a bigger strike farther up the creek. Jack, Claudio, and Joaquín paused to talk awhile, then accepted their advice to move on and rode away.

Out of sight, they doubled back through the woods and met up with the band. Joaquín gave a description of the place and divided the band in half, so that they could attack both sides of the creek at the same time. The orders were simple. Each man was to choose one or two of the miners that he would be responsible for and kill. They would wait, hidden within sight of the quarry, until all were in position and until they heard the cry: *Yo soy Joaquín*. That was the signal to attack.

It was all over in five minutes. The miners never even had a chance to reach for their guns after being startled by that strident cry, which would terrorize the gold fields from Shasta to the Mexican line for three more years.

"Yo soy Joaquín!"

Fourteen dead *Americanos*. Only two of them were Frenchmen who had sailed across the wide Atlantic to find better luck in a new land. And one was an Irishman from Boston. And one an Englishman, correspondent for the *London Times*, who had traveled all that distance to die in a land he could only write of with contempt. And one a Dutchman who had left a rich farm in Pennsylvania in the care of wife and children until he got back with gold enough to buy more ground and bring his brothers and parents to this land where men were free. The others were from Philadelphia and New York and Baltimore, from the crowded East, where the news of gold in California had caused an epidemic of fever in the blood.

Joaquín looked about at the bodies lying there in the

final indignity of death. Some lay in the water where they had been working, one over a sluicing rocker he and a partner had built, some on the creek bank where they had made some last feeble efforts to fight back.

Was he bandit or patriot, killer or revolutionary? Joaquín wondered. Was such killing justified because he had a motive? Was vengeance ever a proper cause?

Antonia broke his daydream. "The gold!" she cried. "Look at the gold!"

The others had searched through the tents and belongings of the miners and found their caches. Antonia had ordered them to put it all in one pile.

Joaquín turned to look at the growing mound of gold.

Pickle jars and fruit cans full of dust, sacks of nuggets, and buckets half full of rich placer gold; it was a fortune.

He glanced again at the dead bodies, wondering, but was hailed by the excited members of his band as they found other pokes and brought them to the pile. Forget the questions, he told himself. Bandit or patriot, what did it matter? He was their leader. The decisions were up to him and the safety and welfare of these men, of Antonia, were his first responsibility.

The gold? The gold rightfully belonged to Mexico. It was Mexican gold; not for *Americanos* but for Mexicans.

He strode to the pile and, with his booted foot, pushed part of it to one side, dividing the pile in half.

"Claudio," he called, "pack this half of the gold and put it on my horse." He looked around at the members of his band, men and women, who were hovering expectantly around the divided pile of gold. "The other half we will share," he told them. "There

105

are twenty of us. Antonia will divide it into twenty equal parts. One for each of us."

"Joaquín, we do not like this. It is too much that you keep half and divide the rest with us."

"*Amigo,*" said Joaquín in a soft voice, "I get one share, even as you. The other half I set aside is for Mexico. We will distribute it to our countrymen who have suffered at the hands of these terrible *Americanos*, even as you and I. We will give it to the church, or send it back to Mexico to be given to the poor, or to finance an army to fight the Yankees."

"No!"

The speaker spoke for all. The gang talked excitedly among themselves. Most of them disagreed with their leader.

"It is our gold," one of them argued. "Did we not kill for it?"

"Yes, we had to kill," said Joaquín regretfully. "But it is not for the gold that we kill. What are we—bandits? Are we no better than the terrible *Americanos* whom we are fighting?"

The gold fever was on them. They would not listen to reason. One of them grabbed up a sack of nuggets.

"*Sí! Banditos!*" he cried, laughing as he turned to the others in the band and waved the sack. "I kill! I take!"

A shot startled the group into silence. The bandito's hat flew off. He dropped the bag of gold and spun around to face Joaquín who stood in a crouched position, gun in hand.

Joaquín was smiling a cold, brittle smile. He blew on the barrel of his gun as he stood erect. "I am not so good a shot yet, eh, Hermando?'' he said laughing. Then, with eyes cold, he said, ''I meant to put that bullet in your head. Next time I will.''

Addressing the group, he said, ''Who rides with Joaquín, rides for Mexico. Ours is a noble cause. Our purpose is to drive the Yankees out of California, and to reclaim the gold which rightfully belongs to Mexico. We are not bandits. We are patriots!''

There was no disagreement within the band this time. The men shrugged and lifted hands in a gesture of acceptance. They nodded, saying, ''Patriots . . . noble cause . . . *bueno!*

Joaquín indicated to Antonia to divide the half of the gold for the members of the band. Then, pointing to the other half, he said to Claudio, ''Pack it.''

He turned away, walked a few steps to a log, and sat down. He sat there watching the activity, wondering where this course of events would lead. He could say, ''patriot,'' but the *Americanos* would say, ''bandit, killer.'' This news would travel through the gold fields and, from this day on, Murrieta would be a marked man; marked for an outlaw's death. Every stranger that he met would be an enemy, a potential danger. It was all so different from what he had planned his life to be. He bowed his head, covered his eyes with his hands, and prayed a silent prayer for forgiveness and strength.

The gold had been divided. The horses had been brought up. The band was ready to leave. Three-Fingered Jack brought his own horse and Joaquín's to the log. He was swinging a loop of something. With a strange smile, he offered it to Joaquín.

Joaquín stood. He took it to see what it was and recoiled in horror. It was a rawhide thong, knotted into

107

a loop in which were strung fourteen human ears. Joaquín threw it from him.

Jack picked it up and hung it from the pommel of Joaquín's saddle. "No, my *capitan*. You keep this. It is to let all know that Murrieta, the Avenger, was here."

Joaquín was facing Jack, trying to find words to express his revulsion. He looked around at the dead bodies, each one with an ear missing, blood running from the wounds. Jack was speaking calmly. "From now on, my *capitan*, we live by fear. The more the *Americanos* fear us, the safer we are. Wherever we strike, we will leave this mark of Murrieta so that the *Americanos* will fear Murrieta as they fear death itself."

Some of the gang had ridden up to see what was going on. They cheered what Three-Fingers had said. There was a certain logic in it, Joaquín had to admit. Again, he had to agree with what his heart told him was wrong. He looked around at the men of his band. They were a hard, rough lot, victimized by fate, despoiled by the *Americanos*; all men who had risked life, who knew the meaning of fear, the power of fear. His glance held on Antonia, and she nodded in agreement.

How strange, how different, how like a nightmare life could turn—the reverse of the life one planned and endeavored to achieve. How devious and unexpected were the twists and sudden turns of destiny. Murrieta, the Avenger, was not a person that the gentle Joaquín—lover, horse trainer, family man, and faithful husband —would ever have even wanted to know. Murrieta, the Avenger, was a person Joaquín could never like.

But like him or not, Murrieta was the leader. Joaquín

108

grasped the horn of his saddle, avoiding the touch of the bloody knotted thong, and swung into the seat.

He waved one arm forward. *"Vamos!"* he cried and pressed spurs to his horse.

Four raids later, the band had doubled in numbers, to about forty members, with a greater proportion of men. They had an unwieldy amount of gold. Too much to keep unprotected in several packing boxes in the office of the Fandango house in Hornitos.

This was the half held back from the raiders and they loaded it in a wagon and the four of them—Joaquín, Antonia, Jack, and Claudio, with others of the gang— went into Merced which was on the old Spanish trail running north and south through the San Joaquín valley.

The fame of Murrieta had spread and they were greeted by a mob in the plaza in front of the church. They handed out gold to everyone. It was Mexico's gold, for their countrymen here as well as for those in Mexico.

The priest came out to watch the milling, shouting throng of his parishioners. Joaquín noticed him, standing beside the door of the mission, and walked over.

"Buenos dias, padre."

"Good day, my son."

"It has been a long winter and I have given no confession, *padre*."

The priest nodded his tonsured head. "Come in, my son."

He opened the heavy oaken door and held it while Joaquín removed his hat and stepped into the gloom and peaceful silence of the church.

As the door closed, shutting off the shaft of sunlight, the priest said, "I am Father Cordova."

Joaquín went down on one knee to kiss the priest's hand. He said, "I am Joaquín Carillo, holy father."

"Rise." The priest caught Joaquín's hand and drew him to his feet. "Do not call me holy; I am a man like yourself. There is none holy, only the Father in heaven and his son, Jesus Christ."

"*Sí, padre.*"

"And you lie. You are Murrieta."

"*Sí, padre.*"

Sadly, Joaquín thought, how true; that the real Joaquín Carillo did no longer exist, only Murrieta. Again he had to agree with what his heart told him was wrong. Because there was still a Joaquín Carillo in his heart. If only he could find a place, a time, a way, that Joaquín Carillo might live again.

The priest led him to the door of the confessional booth. Joaquín entered and sat, hat in hand, in the tiny booth and felt the seriousness and sacredness of this moment, face to face with God. Always before, a confession had been of minor sins; of pride, of thoughtlessness, of selfishness, of omission. Now Murrieta's sins were of a magnitude that staggered him.

His thoughts were interrupted by the voice of the priest, behind the grille, intoning the invitation to confess.

"Father, my sins are beyond forgiveness."

"Praise God! You recognize the sin. Too many will not see what they do as evil, or they qualify it with reason." The voice of Father Cordova was like a soothing balm. "God is speaking to you, my son. Directing you to better ways. You must stop this killing and theft and violence.''

Joaquín pressed palms to his forehead. This soothing balm had no power to heal. There could be no peace in confessing what must continue. Murrieta was not of God, but of satan. Murrieta had no right in a church. Murrieta defamed this holy ground. Joaquín jammed his hat on and started to leave. Then shouted back at the grille.

''It is not killing—but retribution!''

'' 'Vengeance is mine, said the Lord.' It is not for you to deliver retribution, my son,'' said the soothing voice from behind the grille.

''Then who?'' shouted Joaquín. ''Who else will do it? Mexico has been wronged. My people have been wronged. Who else will right that wrong, if I don't?''

He was outside the confessional box, talking back through the open door to the man behind the grille. Not speaking to God. Not even speaking to a priest. But repeating the arguments they had proclaimed all winter; he and Jack and Claudio, and all the other members of the gang.

He started away, to get out of this holy place which made him feel uncomfortable, but a hand caught him and yanked him around. Strong hands held him. It was Father Cordova.

''You must stop this bloodshed, Murrieta! Stop this killing and stealing!''

''I do not steal!'' Joaquín shouted at the priest. ''I have nothing! What gold I had was stolen from me! And my brother and cousins slaughtered for their gold!

111

I am reclaiming the gold for Mexico, to whom it rightfully belongs. It is your gold, *padre*—our gold—Mexico's gold. I take it only to return it to the rightful owners—our people.''

Father Cordova shook him gently. His eyes held Joaquín's with their intensity. '' 'Give unto Caesar that which is Caesar's.' My son, I plead with you, not for justice, not for what is right, but for your immortal soul.''

Joaquín tore himself free. ''I have no soul, *padre*. These terrible *Americanos* beat me to death. They left me for dead. My body lived, but my soul died at their hands. I have no more soul than the cougar in the forest. I don't belong in this place. It was wrong for me to come here.'' He started up the aisle to the door.

''Joaquín . . . at first you said your name was Joaquín.''

Joaquín stopped. Without turning, he said, *''Sí. Yo soy Joaquín*. But that is only our battle cry. I am Murrieta!''

Father Cordova caught him at the door.

''I beg you, in the name of common sense, stop this evil thing you are doing. These *Americanos* are stronger than us. There are too many. We cannot fight them. If you keep this up, they will retaliate and kill us all.''

''No, *padre*,'' said Murrieta, looking at the priest with eyes of icy hardness. ''They will learn to fear Murrieta. For every one of my countrymen they slay, I will slay two of them. We are small now, but we will be an army. It is the *Americanos* who will be driven from Alta, California. This land will be Mexico's once more.''

He yanked open the door and strode out into the blinding sunlight of the plaza. Father Cordova stood in the open doorway, watched him for a moment, then clasped his hands at his chest, bowed his head until his lips touched the laced fingers, and closed his eyes in prayer.

Joaquín walked to the Fandango house, where the wagon and horses were tied. He went inside and signaled Jack and Claudio.

"We are leaving," he said. "Claudio, you take three of the men with you. The four of you should be enough to get the gold to Mexico safely. Never ride together. One man driving the wagon. One far in front, but within gunshot. And two far behind."

To Three-Fingered Jack, he said, "We are going up into the hills. Away from Hornitos. We need more men." He nodded back toward the Fandango house. "See if you can get some of these to ride with us. Good men, who will fight the *gringo*, to drive him out of California."

Jack nodded and left. Claudio said, "Send someone else. I want to be with you."

Joaquín looked at this cousin, this friend of his youth who was closer than a brother, this twin with the freckles and green eyes. Impulsively, he clasped Claudio to his bosom with a hug and a kiss. Then held him at arm's length.

"Claudio, you and Antonia are the only ones I can trust. I cannot let Antonia leave me. So you are the only one who can get this gold to my father who will know what to do with it. You tell him. Some must go to our people, and some to the government to build an army to recapture California."

113

Claudio shrugged and lifted both hands in agreement. It was plain he did not like it, but would do a good job. Joaquín hugged him again, then slapped his shoulder.

"Vaya con Dios."

Looking around, Joaquín said, "Now to find my Antonia."

Across the plaza he saw a store with a sign, "Millinery," and he started toward it. As he passed, he saw Father Cordova still standing in the doorway of the church in the attitude of prayer. Joaquín shut that vision from his mind and walked a little faster.

Chapter 10

"That is the Captain Roberts, the one in the military uniform, at the table playing cards with the one called Bull Dutton. I will capture these two," Joaquín whispered.

He was laying out the plan of attack as he, Antonia, and Three-Fingered Jack crouched behind the stack of logs he had felled last year, logs with which he was going to build a cabin for their home. They were back at their old claim on the Stanislaus River. The pile of logs was still there. The table he had built was still here. And the same men who had ravished Rosita, now Antonia, and driven them from this claim were back again.

"The one dowstream, panning, is the man named Harvey," continued Joaquín. "Antonia, you take him."

"The two at the sluice are Christian and John Little. They are for you, Jack."

Joaquín glanced around at his two partners to be sure they understood. They both nodded and he said, "Get closer, wait for my signal, and try not to shoot. I want them alive."

Joaquín waited as Antonia and Jack moved off into

the trees to get into position. He had not brought any of the band because this was a special raid that he wanted for himself, Three-Fingered Jack, and Antonia, alone. These men, these former Regulators, had been the cause of all his sorrow and anguish. These men were the instigators of all the upheaval in his own life and in this land. These were the terrible *Americanos* who were despoiling Alta California, claiming the gold, killing his countrymen. These men he meant to deal with in a special way; they would not die easily.

"*Yo soy Joaquín!*"

The cry signaled the attack. Joaquín had his gun in Sam Roberts' back before the man could get up from the table. He took the gun from Roberts' holster and backed off, holding the two at gunpoint, as Antonia marched Harvey up from the creek and Jack brought the other two to the table. Roberts had been the only one armed.

Joaquín held them there, with his two guns, while Jack tied their hands and Antonia found their guns and gold. There had been some talk at first from Roberts, cursing his men for not wearing their guns, until Joaquín stopped it by rapping the Captain's face with a gun barrel. Then Three-Fingered Jack gathered the horses and tied the feet of each man after he was in the saddle.

All mounted now, with Antonia leading the way and Jack and Joaquín riding behind the file of captives, they started back to their hideout in the High Sierras.

Climbing constantly, Antonia led the line of captives to a plateau high in the Sierra Nevada mountains. There appeared to be no trail, but finally she led them over a crest to which clung a scattering of stunted, wind-gnarled pine trees. The camp was there.

Instantly, they were surrounded by a noisy crowd of men, and some women dressed as men, who welcomed them with loud greetings and excited whoops and much laughter and back-slapping. Throughout the camp, women who were cooking or doing other chores, and men on guard duty, called and waved. There were about eighty in the band now.

This camp was a natural fortress. The rock-strewn mesa, a mile in length and half as wide, was accessible on only one side. The other side was a sheer precipice, a drop of sixty feet or more to a swirling mountain stream which was the north fork of the Tuolumne River.

As they dismounted, Joaquín ordered that the captives be tied to separate trees in a clump of pines at the far end of the camp. Then, while they had a refreshing drink in the shade in front of the tent he and Antonia shared, Joaquín told the curious members of the band why he had not taken them on this raid.

"These are the leaders of the Regulators," he explained for those who did not already know. "Or sometimes they're called the Hounds. And the one with the long, horse face, dressed in that Army uniform, he is the Captain Roberts who is their commander."

Then he told the band the entire story from the time they had first met these *Americanos* at their claim on the Stanislaus River and his young wife, Rosita, the woman they now knew as Antonia, had invited these strangers to supper. It was a long and gory story, the kind of true-life story the emotional Mexicans love to tell over a campfire, or in the *cantina*. It was the first time Joaquín had ever taken them into his confidence or revealed the other side of his character.

Most of these men and women who rode with him knew Murrieta only as their fearless, relentless, and impassive leader. Most of them had felt the sting of *gringo* injustice and violence. They rode with him not because they were patriots, not for any idealistic cause, but for the gold they plundered and for retaliation against the *gringo* spoilers at whose hands they had suffered.

Rough and tough and self-seeking as were these men, they listened to him with tears in their eyes, loving him with a far greater loyalty, as they suffered with the young Joaquín and his child-bride, Rosita.

At the end, Joaquín said, "These I had to capture myself, with my Antonia." And he held Antonia by the hand as the band cheered and wiped their eyes.

"For these I have planned a special execution," Joaquín continued. "But first, a fiesta. We will celebrate this victory with food and wine and music."

More cheers.

"Then we will see how these Regulators like a taste of Mexican justice."

More cheers, and the men and women came and hugged him, and kissed Antonia, and vowed their loyalty anew.

Always in a Mexican camp there is guitar music, someone who blows a horn, and one who beats a drum or maracas or clavas. Always there is wine and women and gambling. Now, while antelope, deer, and sides of beef were basting on spits over open fires, the women brought corn cakes and other food to serve the men as they drank, played cards, and talked and danced with the women serving them to the music of a *mariani* band.

Then, as the meat and beans were almost ready to be eaten, most of the women changed from the pants and shirt they wore on the trail into dresses they had hidden in their belongings. Tortoise-shell combs were put into new hair styles and *mantillas* worn to drape a face tinted with cosmetics, the cheeks rouged, the eyes shadowed, the lips carmined, until the men barely recognized these women with whom they had been riding in the raids of Murrieta.

Antonia, of all the women, did not dress. She bathed and changed into a clean pair of toreador pants and bolero jacket, but her hair was cut short. It could not be styled any other way; it would not hold a tortoise-shell comb. She was Antonia, the spirit of vengeance. Nothing could change that until the hated *Americano*, Captain Roberts, had paid in full with his blood.

She and Joaquín and Three-Fingered Jack sat in front of their tent, drinking the wine, laughing and talking, flushed with a sense of victory. The capture of the Regulators gave Joaquín a sense of fulfillment, although it was a malevolent sense of satisfaction, tinged with regret because it brought memories of his older brother, Jésus, and the two older cousins, who were all gone. So it was with mingled joy and sadness that Joaquín watched his friends and compatriots revel in this victory.

As night fell, and the food was all eaten, the wine all drunk, and most of the men had taken their women to their beds, in tents or in blankets under the stars, Joaquín said to Three-Fingered Jack: "You check on those Regulators. Make sure they're all tied securely and post a guard. I don't want one of my drunken followers to stab them in the night out of loyalty to me. I want them alive to suffer when we execute them in the morning.''

The high plateau was strewn with rocks, some of them big enough for a man to hide behind, others the size of a fruit jar. It was among these rocks that Joaquín laid out a course, the next morning, where a horse could run freely and at high speed.

With several of the others, including Antonia, he saddled and mounted his horse. Then had Three-Fingered Jack untie the Regulators from the trees and bring them to the course. With their hands securely tied behind them, the *Americanos* stood with scowling, fearful faces, wondering what this crazy greaser kid had in store for them.

As the captives and the band watched expectantly, Joaquín threw his lariat over the fat one, Bull Dutton, and with the rope looped in a half hitch over the pommel of his saddle, he urged his horse into a walk, then a trot.

As he was pulled along, Bull Dutton fought the rope at first, then ran to keep from falling, stumbling on the rocks underfoot. As Joaquín spurred his mount to a gallop, Bull Dutton lost his footing and fell. His body bounced back and forth against the rocks like a gold nugget in a rocker.

When Joaquín raced back to the starting point, the sack of flesh he dragged behind his horse was unrecognizable, except that it had been a man.

The men of the band had cheered at the start. Now, as they looked down at this battered pulp, with the skull split open, the brains and the guts of the body hanging out in a tangle of white cords and bloody organs, all muddy and brown with the dust of the mesa, they fell silent.

Joaquín looked at the other mounted men. "Who will take the next one?" he called.

They avoided his eyes. They scowled and looked away. They looked down at the bloody remains on the ground and closed their eyes. They checked their reins. They readjusted their stirrups. The *Americanos* struggled to break free, but were held there, waiting their turn, by strong hands.

Joaquín smiled dispassionately, looking from the Regulators to the mounted members of his band. He untied the rope from his pommel. Then he took a new lariat, cast it over John Little, and drew him from the line of *Americanos*.

"This is the one who first raped my young wife, my little dove, my Rosita. The woman you now know as Antonia." He pointed down at the remains of Bull Dutton. "That one"—then he pointed to the other Regulators—"all of them. They took turns raping her, beating her when she fought back, and forced me to watch while they desecrated my bride."

He glanced at the mounted men of the band, then down at the others, and continued. "You think this is cruel?" Then he answered himself. "I think it is too good for them! I think only the devil in hell will have a proper punishment for these Regulators."

He held up his end of the rope that was tied around the cringing John Little.

"Now who of you will take this one?"

They were all willing, all reached for the rope, but

Joaquín handed it to Antonia, saying, "It is fitting that you kill this one."

The band cheered. Antonia spurred her horse to an immediate gallop. John Little never had a chance to run. He was jerked from his feet where he stood. Antonia ran the course and dragged a bloody corpse back to a cheering crowd.

Finally only Captain Roberts was left. Joaquín threw a loop over the man. "This one I must kill myself," he said. "It is a vow I have made."

The men were excited. The sight of blood incites passion. Mexican passions run hot, and the band was milling about and yelling now. Some struck at Roberts in order to have a personal hand in his death. They ripped his uniform.

Then, suddenly, Roberts tore the lariat from his body. Somehow he had gotten his hands free. He pulled one of the mounted men from his horse and leaped into the saddle. The others reached for him, but couldn't hold him. He kicked at his mount and the horse bolted. The mounted members of the gang, spurring and kicking their horses, followed in close pursuit.

Joaquín put spurs to his horse. Roberts was away and running. But the only way he could run was toward the far side of the plateau.

The chase was short. The horse Roberts was riding knew of the precipice and stopped short. Roberts went over the horse's head. He scrambled to his feet and saw the swirling waters of the stream so far below. He looked back at the band of riders closing on him, hesitated only a second, and jumped.

One of the men was there quickly enough to see Roberts hit the water and disappear. When Joaquín looked down, there was no sign of the man, only the turbulent water.

When they got back to the group at the camp, Antonia was still sitting on her horse. The other riders shouted to the crowd: "He is dead! No one could live through such a fall! It had to kill him! It was suicide!"

Joaquín sat apart. When Antonia looked at him, he lifted his hands and eyebrows in an eloquent gesture of uncertainty.

"Who knows?" he said.

Antonia could not possibly have heard him amid all the noise and loud voices and confusion, but she got the message. She dismounted and went into their tent. Joaquín sat there in the saddle, watching that closed tent flap. He sensed Antonia's feeling of defeat. He felt his own disappointment and shame, that he had failed. Then a new movement caught his attention and, in an agony of frustration, he watched Three-Fingered Jack cut off the ears of the dead *Americanos* and add them to the loop.

Only four where there should have been five.

Chapter 11

With each successful raid, the reputation of Murrieta spread farther throughout the length and breadth of the land. By word of mouth and by newspaper articles in the San Francisco papers, the name of the Avenger struck fear. These accounts were never given by survivors, but only by those who had discovered a mining camp wiped out, all the men dead, each with one ear severed, the gold and weapons and horses all gone.

Constantly on the move now, the band robbed stage coaches and wagon trains, held up businesses and banks owned by the *Americanos*, and shared the stolen gold with their persecuted countrymen who called Murrieta their patron and protector.

Because of the fame and fear that preceded them the band traveled openly. And in that summer of the year, 1851, Murrieta, Antonia, Jack, and Claudio led a group of about ten riders into the town of French Flat, on the south fork of the American River in the northern gold fields. They were foraging to replenish food supplies for the main body of the band, which was temporarily camped back in the hills.

Riding in front of the group, with Claudio at his side,

Joaquín paused as they passed an alley off of the main street. He held up a hand for silence and they listened to strange, low sounds coming from the alley.

"What is this?" Joaquín asked, urging his mount into the alley. The others followed.

The alley was made up of about six boxlike buildings, three on each side, each with a door which had a barred opening. As they moved past the doors, bare young arms extended, beckoning. Slanting eyes peered from behind the bars and high-pitched voices set up a singsong chant.

"China girl velle nice. You comee inside, please?"

"You fadda, he just been here!"

"Two bitee lookee, fo bitee feelee, six bitee to go in!"

Joaquín moved his mount to look through the barred opening of the first door. The Chinese girl whose arm reached out through the bars smiled at him, lifted the black silk blouse which covered her upper body, and leered.

"China girl velle nice, you see? Givee much pleasure!"

The girl was nothing more than a child, perhaps eleven or twelve years old. Behind her, sitting on a bench, their backs against the wall of the crib, were five other girls ranging in age from ten years to maybe fourteen.

"My turn next," the girl at the opening said. "You likee? You wantee see more?"

Joaquín was dumbfounded. He looked around at the others. Three-Fingered Jack, Claudio, and others of the men were looking in at the other cribs. Antonia was sitting her horse at the entrance to the alley, watching soberly.

The men started laughing and whooping, calling to each other to share what they had discovered.

Joaquín dismounted and led his horse to Antonia. "You wait here. Keep out of this."

He walked back to the first cell and tried the door. It was locked. He backed off and kicked at it. As he was getting set for another kick, a Chinese in a black pajama-suit came running from the main street, with short shuffling steps.

"Wait, please! Me open!"

As the Chinese approached Joaquín, he bowed, saying, "Six bitee, please."

Joaquín looked at him severely. Five other Chinese, dressed in the same black costumes, were coming from the main street, running with short steps, calling, "We open!"

Each went to a separate door and stood bowing, saying, "Six bitee, please."

The riders burst into raucous laughter, slapping and hugging each other, until Joaquín caught the first Chinese by his queue, calling, "Claudio! Jack! Get 'em!"

In the dusty alley, with the girls all reaching through the barred openings and calling enticements, amid the milling horses as the riders dismounted, they gathered the six Chinese. Joaquín tied their queues together in one knot, then held it high, while Three-Fingered Jack methodically prepared to slit their throats.

The Chinese procurers knelt, begging mercy, profoundly puzzled that a proper business arrangement had brought them to this end. As Jack slit the last yellow throat, Joaquín released his hold of the topknot and the six bodies collapsed in a bloody heap.

Joaquín pointed in a sweeping gesture to the six cribs. "Turn 'em loose! Break down those doors," he ordered.

With whoops and yells of excitement, the men kicked in and battered down the doors. From each of the six cells came from four to six Chinese "boat girls." They were children eight to fourteen years old, imported from China and sold in the slave market in San Francisco's Chinatown to the masters or owners of cribs and parlor houses.

They all wore the traditional clothing of the trade, a black silk blouse with a narrow embroidered band of flowers which edged the neckline in front and back. Some were clad in black, silken pantaloons and short stubby shoes, but most were in their bare feet and wore only a blouse that rarely reached below the hips.

Thirty Chinese children, twelve horses, the men of the band, and the bloody mound of six dead Chinese pimps were crowded together there in the ten-foot-wide dusty alley. Out on the main street, where Antonia still sat her mount and held Joaquín's horse, some of the townspeople had gathered to see what was going on.

In the alley, the girls who knew only one way of life sang their singsong seductions. Some of them raised their blouses to display their wares. Some more aggressive went after the men, trying to pull down their pants and drag them into the cribs.

An older one, maybe fourteen, came over to the heap of dead pimps. She looked at the gruesome sight with passive dismay. She stood with her tiny feet tightly together, her hands clasped to her elbows at her waist in a slightly bowed posture. Her smooth, poreless, dolllike face was inscrutable as she glanced from the bloody heap up at Joaquín.

"Ah, poor master is no more. Who will feed us?"

"You are free!" said Joaquín.

"Flee?" said the child, slanted, puzzled eyes looking up at the slim Mexican youth who was her savior.

"Yes, free!" Joaquín waved one hand to indicate the main street of the town and the surrounding hills. "You can go."

He saw she did not understand, so he said, "Go anywhere!" He waved his hand again to the distant hills. "You are free!"

Eyes cast down demurely in her doll face, the girl shook her head. "Me no flee," she said in her high-pitched voice. Then smiling at him and nodding in a slight bow, "You Melican. You are flee."

"I am not *Americano!*" stated Joaquín. "I am Mexican!"

"Soo, soo," she chanted, singsong. "Flee man all Melican. China girl all slave. Mei Toy no flee. Mei Toy hongly."

Joaquín looked around for help. Antonia was still sitting her mount at the entrance to the alley. He saw that his men had succumbed to the overt Oriental offering. Some were allowing themselves to be dragged into the cribs. Others were coming out, hitching up their breeches and buckling on gunbelts. Some of the girls were displaying gold pieces. Proudly, they showed the shiny slugs to the other girls and talked in high, excited, singsong tones.

Mei Toy was pulling at his sleeve. "Come see, come see," she cried, slanted eyes dancing. "Mei Toy give you much pleasure.'' She was trying to pull him toward one of the cribs as she made seductive motions with her frail, undernourished body.

Joaquín resisted.

She caught him by the gunbelt, pulling. ''Come see! Make you feel good. Velly good. Then you be my master.''

Joaquín held back, looking around for help. Three-Fingered Jack was howling with laughter. Claudio spread his hands in a helpless gesture as one of the children dragged him toward one of the shattered doors.

Jaoquín beat at the girl with his hat. He twisted her hands off his belt.

''No!'' he cried. ''You are free! *Vaya!* Go!''

Mei Toy's lips curved down in dejection. Almond eyes filled with tears. She stood, tiny feet pressed together, hands clasped to forearms at her waist, head bowed, and said, pleading, ''Give much pleasure. Mei Toy good girl.''

Joaquín jammed his hat back on. ''*Sí, sí*, you good girl. Velly good girl,'' he said, trying to talk in Spanish-Chinese-English and placate this unhappy child. ''Me no want your pleasure.''

The girl hung her head in shame. Her thin shoulders shook with weeping.

He tried to explain. ''All I did was set you free. You owe me nothing. Just go! Why you no go?''

Some of the men gathered around, attracted by Jack's laughter and the argument.

''Ah, give her a try, *Capitan*,'' said one of the men, snickering.

''Sure, Joaquín, try her out,'' another added. ''This

129

Chinee ass ain't no different than other women. They don't run sideways."

The men whooped and slapped each other and pushed Joaquín toward the girl.

Mei Toy brightened. She caught his belt again. "China girl velee nice. You fadda, he likes me," she said in her singsong voice. "You see now. Come inside, please?"

Joaquín yanked himself free. He turned around and shoved his men aside roughly and they clutched at each other for support as they howled with laughter. Then he turned back to the crestfallen girl, who stood with tiny feet pressed tightly together, miserable in her rejection.

"Go! Go!" he yelled.

"You no like Mei Toy?"

"No! I mean, yes, I like Mei Toy."

Bowed head now lifted, she smiled seductively. "Then you let Mei Toy make you feel hoppy?"

"NO!"

"Mei Toy make you feel velly good."

"NO! I do feel good!" Joaquín yelled. "And I am happy!" He made a grotesque smile and pointed to his face. "See? Me velly hoppy!"

"Melican fonee," said the poor, puzzled child. "Say feel hoppy when mad."

"I'm not mad! And I am not *Americano*!"

"Then you like Mei Toy?"

"*Sí*! I like. I like."

"Then you be Mei Toy's master?"

"No!" cried Joaquín in despair. "I set you free!"

Tears filled those almond eyes. "Ah, poor Mei Toy," sang the girl, rocking in her misery. "No master. Nobody to give pleasure. Nobody to make feel good. Nobody to feed her.''

Later that day, Joaquín stood in the shade on the veranda of the saloon and watched as the rest of his followers moved into French Flat.

His decision to take over the town had been influenced by the presence of the Chinese harlots. Antonia had said that the townspeople would drive them into the wilderness to starve. Which was probably true. Or that the miners would rape and ravish the helpless children to death. In the gold fields the Chinese were treated even worse than were the Spanish-speaking people.

Joaquín watched as a remuda of fine horses were herded down the main street into a corral behind the livery stable. Beyond the one main street of French Flat, the South Fork of the American River flashed blue and silver in the sun. There were no miners working there. The town seemed deserted except for the men and women of his own band. The many townspeople, who had watched the slaughter of the Chinese masters, had disappeared. The houses and stores were shuttered, the doors closed, the blinds drawn. Only the saloon had not had time to close up.

Following the herd of horses came the married men of the band and their wives, riding in spring wagons with their children piled in back. Behind the families came the supply wagons, now almost empty of food and ammunition.

There were about eighty men and women in the band now. Three-Fingered Jack had divided them into groups, or squads, of twenty, with a lieutenant responsible for the men and women in his group. It was getting to be an army.

Antonia, who was standing beside him on the veranda, said, "Look at those shameless children." She was talking about the Chinese harlots who were plying their trade, the only thing they knew, amid the idle men. "You should have let them alone."

Joaquín nodded agreement. But it was too late now. He felt a responsibility for these child-whores since it had been his noble act which set them free.

"Let 'em stay," said Claudio. "The men will enjoy them. We'll have a holiday."

"Forget them!" said Three-Fingered Jack. "We get our supplies—what we came for—and ride on."

Antonia was amused by this new complication, but truly concerned for these innocent children. "But if we go on, they will try to follow us and they'll die in the wilderness," she said.

"Better to die free in the open, than to die in a crib," said Jack.

Joaquín, who had never enjoyed the responsibilities of command, felt a growing impatience. "It's all my fault," he said sharply. "I'll take care of them."

"*Bueno!*" said Antonia. She glanced around at Claudio, giving him a wink. "Then I will not worry about them. Instead, I'll find some place to get a hot bath." She stepped out of the shade of the veranda, calling to another woman.

Joaquín watched her leave, then took command.

"Jack, get the squad leaders. One squad is to search for gold. Another for guns and ammunition. Another for food."

Three-Fingered Jack nodded.

"You go with the last squad and clear out all the townspeople. They may leave with whatever they can carry on their person—no horses or wagons—or they can die here."

As Jack moved away Joaquín turned to his twin cousin, put an arm across his shoulders, and led him into the saloon. "You're right, Claudio," he said. "We need a rest. We'll stay here a few days. The men can have a holiday and enjoy themselves."

The barroom was empty except for a bartender and two saloon girls. As Claudio and Joaquín sat at a table made from a packing crate, the bartender left the girls, who were talking in fearful whispers at one end of the bar, and approached them.

"What'll it be, gents?"

"A bottle and two glasses—whatever you have," said Joaquín.

The bartender brought a bottle and glasses, set them on the table, and said, "That'll be fifteen dollars or one ounce of gold."

Joaquín looked up, smiling. The bartender was a big man, an Irishman from Boston, who had braved the emigrant trail to make his fortune. He had a florid complexion and luxuriant handlebar mustache. Still smiling, Joaquín placed a twenty-dollar gold slug on the table. As the bartender dug in the pocket of his apron to make change, Joaquín raised one hand.

"Keep it."

The bartender nodded, took the coin, and started back to the bar.

"*Yo soy Joaquín.*"

The big Irishman froze. He turned to face the two men at the table, his eyes bulging with fearful awareness. He inhaled a deep breath and stood tall.

"I thought so. The one known as Murrieta?" he said evenly.

"*Sí*. Do not be brave, *señor*," said Joaquín. "Most of the townspeople have already fled. Take your girls and go in peace."

The two girls came from the bar. One of them grabbed the bartender and started pulling him toward the door. He tore himself free and faced the two men at the table.

"This is my place," he stated. "I built it with these two hands. It's all I've got. Now, I'll serve you two guests, like gentlemen. Or *you* can go." He slapped the twenty-dollar gold slug down on the table and stood towering over them.

"What'll it be, gents?"

Joaquín sighed. He could feel nothing but admiration and respect for so brave a man. Too often in warfare, when it is reduced to individual rivals, face to face, you find yourself liking the enemy and disliking yourself for what must be done. This was one more time when he must do what his heart told him was wrong.

"But I am Murrieta," he tried once more.

"And I am Timothy O'Leary!"

Joaquín closed his eyes and shook his head sadly. Casually, he leaned back in his chair, pulled a derringer from his belt, and fired pointblank into the man's aproned belly.

The Irishman's eyes widened with disbelief at the impact. He rose on tiptoe, clutching at his stomach, then crumpled to the floor. The girls screamed and darted through the doorway.

Joaquín arose. He looked down at the big Irishman as he replaced the gun in his belt. His young face twisted in an ugly grimace of weariness and regret. Remorse tore his guts like a cougar's claws. Heart aching for this courageous man who, somewhere, had family and friends who loved him, Joaquín's mind skirted the brink of madness as he cursed the satanic fate which had chosen him to avenge his people.

Finally, in control again, his face impassive, he stepped around the body of the brave Irishman.

"Claudio, I'll have that drink with you later," he said, and walked out into the bright sunlight of the street.

Chapter 12

"Got all that gold loaded?"

"*Sí*. It is all in two boxes. The boxes are in the wagon."

"*Bueno*. Now get those Chinese girls into the wagon."

Claudio did not answer immediately. He was struggling to repress laughter as he watched Joaquín try on a high beaver hat.

Dressed in business suits, Joaquín and Three-Fingered Jack were taking turns peering at themselves in a small, fly-specked looking glass inside the general store. Antonia made some last adjustments to their bow ties and starched white collars. Then she stepped back to admire these two in their *gringo* costumes.

The tight, stiff hat was too much for Joaquín and he threw it aside and put on his battered *sombrero*. In the looking glass he saw that the *sombrero* was all wrong; it ruined the disguise. He decided to go hatless.

Claudio answered at last. "Twenty of those girls is all I can find."

"They're hiding. They don't want to go," said Antonia.

"They've got to go!" said Joaquín.

"Then you'll have to find them," replied Claudio.

Three-Fingered Jack was still at the looking glass, adjusting a brown derby on his head with evident approval. "Where are they?" he asked.

"Where could they hide?" asked Joaquín.

Claudio shrugged. "They're scattered out in the woods somewhere. I don't know."

Three-Fingered Jack turned from the looking glass, where he'd been admiring his appearance as a businessman, and said, "Forget them. They don't wish to leave—so let them stay." He put his arm around Joaquín's shoulders. "Come, *amigo*. We are ready. Let us be off to Sacramento."

Joaquín gave in reluctantly. Those Chinese children were a weight on his conscience. He felt responsible for them, but could not waste the day searching the woods for them.

"*Sí. Vamos!*" He caught Antonia about the waist and the three of them walked out of the general store, arm in arm, into the sunlight of the street.

Most of the men and women of the band were gathered about the loaded wagon, waiting to see them off. Two rifle boxes, full of gold, were hidden amid the mob of weeping, wailing Chinese children huddled together in the bed of the wagon.

As Claudio cracked the whip from the driver's seat and the wagon started to move, Jack and Joaquín mounted their horses. They waved to the noisy crowd. The crowd called good wishes and blessings for a safe return, as the two businessmen, on horseback, moved out following the wagon.

The next day, in late afternoon, Joaquín and Jack

stood with the gambler, William Burns, on the second-story veranda of the Boston House. From this vantage point, they had a view of the burgeoning city of Sacramento, the docks and shipping of the riverfront, and the wide sweep of the Sacramento River to the swampy western shore where a village of shacks and warehouses, called Margaretta, was springing up.

It had been a busy morning. Burns had met them for a breakfast of smoked oysters, steak, and eggs. Burns had arranged passage for the Chinese children on a riverboat leaving for San Francisco. He then took Jack and Joaquín to the bank where he did his own banking and introduced them to the bank officers.

The remainder of the day had been spent in weighing and tallying the gold. Joaquín received two bank drafts, each in excess of thirty thousand dollars. One he cashed into minted gold coins. The other he sent by overland express to his father in Sonora. Mexico's gold was going back to Mexico.

As the three men stood now on the veranda overlooking the activity of the main street and docks, a riverboat arrived and anchored in midstream, because there was no opening at the docks. It was a side paddlewheel boat, the type used for transporting freight and passengers between San Francisco and Sacramento. They watched as the passengers were ferried to the shore in rowboats.

"There will be no passengers going back in that one," said the gambler, Burns.

"And why not?" asked Joaquín.

"It comes each month to transport gold from the three banks here in Sacramento to the Bank of America

138

in San Francisco. From there it will be shipped back to New York City."

Joaquín glanced across at his partner, Three-Fingered Jack.

"And when will it depart?" Joaquín asked the gambler.

"It will unload its cargo of supplies tomorrow," said Burns. "The next day it will load the gold, and depart the following day."

"Three days," said Joaquín, nodding soberly. "And that is its name, there on the paddlewheel, *Estrella del Norte*?"

Burns nodded. "*North Star*," he said, repeating the name in English.

"Is it not dangerous, carrying so much wealth?"

"There are armed guards," said Burns. "The banks take every precaution."

"They should," said Joaquín. "It makes a tempting prize, that load of *gringo* gold."

The gambler, Burns, looked at him suspiciously.

Joaquín smiled disarmingly. "Jack," he said, speaking to his partner, "our business here is completed. Let us pay the bill and depart."

He took the gambler, Burns, by the hand. "Will, *gracias*. Thank you for all your help. You will always be welcome in Murrieta's camp. But we must leave. It is risky for Murrieta to stay here." He grinned as he shook the gambler's hand. "Even though we are dressed as businessmen, like yourself, ours is a most dangerous business. You gamble for money. We gamble our lives."

They were meeting in the saloon in French Flat. The

members of the band had all sampled the barrels of whiskey brought back from Sacramento and each one, man or woman, had received three hundred dollars in gold coin, an equal division of one half the gold that had been exchanged at the bank in Sacramento. There was joy and revelry, but there was dissension, too.

Joaquín, still dressed in his business suit, left the table where he had been sitting with Antonia, Jack, and Claudio and made his way through the boisterous crowd to the bar. There, he upended the barrel of whiskey so that no more drinks could be poured from the tap, and banged on a tin serving tray for attention.

"Compadres!" He raised one hand to silence the jubilant crowd.

When he had their attention, he began to speak.

"You have been told we are leaving this place to-morrow. Some of you do not wish to go. I say you must go—"

His words were lost as the men shouted disagreement.

One of the men, with a drink in one hand and one of the remaining Chinese harlots clinging to his arm, pushed forward.

"Joaquín, *mi capitan*!" he cried. "Why do we not stay?" The man was grinning, friendly, confident that he spoke for most of the members of the band. "Let us enjoy this good life!"

"Miguel," said Joaquín, "our purpose is to regain this land for Mexico."

"Sí, Capitan. And for two years we have followed you. We have ridden dangerous trails. We have killed. We have slept in the wet and cold. We have suffered many things. No!"

Behind him, in the crowd, many voiced agreement.

The spokesman shrugged, spread his hands. "I think," he went on, his face bland, "that the *Americano* is too strong for us. We can never drive him from this land. He is too numerous. We kill one and a hundred more come to replace him."

A chorus of agreement echoed this statement and Joaquín glanced from face to face, trying to search out what was in the hearts of these men. In his own heart was a longing to relinquish this position of leadership, to return to the sunny slopes of Sonora, to the peace of his father's land and the golden horses which he loved.

"Miguel, there is logic in what you say. Only an army can win back this land for Mexico."

"*Sí! Sí!*" The majority of the band broke into raucous agreement.

The spokesman glanced around at the others, encouraged. "It is true," he stated. "Let the *políticos* in Mexico City establish an army, with the gold we have sent them and with men who are trained to make war. I am a peaceful man, a peasant. I have killed enough. These murders weigh heavy on my heart."

Joaquín embraced the man.

"*Amigo*, I respect your feelings. I love you for the loyalty you have shown, the bravery with which you have fought."

"*Capitan*, I would die for you," said the man, through his tears.

In the crowded room, many voices raised, some pledging allegiance to Murrieta and his cause, others ready to quit.

"*Un momento!*"

Antonia pushed through the crowd. Her shrill voice

141

silenced the others. In front of Joaquín, she shoved Miguel aside and spat in his face.

"That for you!" she shrieked. "You were not ravished by the *Americano*! You did not have your family killed, your life ruined! You ride to get gold, to drink, to screw your Chinese whore!" She slapped the doll face of the girl who was still clinging to Miguel's arm, and the child fell back and disappeared in the crowd.

"I ride for vengeance!" Antonia shouted to the hushed room. "To avenge myself and my loved ones who were slaughtered. To avenge my people who are still being mistreated by these terrible *Americanos*."

It was the women of the band who picked up the cry.

"Vengeance!" they screamed. "Vengeance!" And they prodded the men and slapped them and called them cowards.

Joaquín grabbed Antonia and swung her around to face him.

"Enough! These, our *compadres*, are not cowards! These are brave men—and brave women, too!" Suddenly he released her. The anger drained from his face.

Softly, depleted of emotion, he asked, "Antonia, have we not killed enough?"

Antonia stood on tiptoe to press her face toward his, her eyes hostile and bright with challenge. "No, we have not killed enough, not while Captain Roberts, the one who was the cause of my ravishment, still lives! He who slew your brother, this killer of our cousins. He prospers and grows fat, while we ride the hills as outlaws."

She turned to the crowd, challenging all. "Do you

forget so quickly what you have suffered at the hands of the *gringos*?''

Then she turned back to Joaquín. ''And you ask if we have not killed enough . . . NO! Never enough, until I see your hands red with the blood of this Captain Roberts!''

The women cheered and some of the men were prodded into echoing those cheers.

Joaquín stepped back, away from the heat of Antonia's fury and the piercing truth of her words. He swiped one hand across his face and looked out upon the now silent crowd.

Quietly, he addressed them. ''I have never, and I will not now, force any of you to ride with me, but you must leave this place. Immediately! It is too close to Sacramento. It is dangerous for you to remain here.''

He took Antonia's hand and put her arm through his as he continued. ''We leave within the hour for Hornitos. There you will be safe from the *Americanos*. If you want my protection, come with us.''

Two hours later, when they assembled to depart, only about half the band joined them. The others had remained in the saloon drinking and arguing and qualifying their decision to remain.

As Joaquín gave the signal to move out, shouting, *''Vamos!''* the dissidents left the barrels in the saloon to trail behind the loyal followers of Murrieta, restating their all too valid reasons for deserting, and crying prayers of farewell.

It was a sad and tearful parting.

Chapter 13

At the close of the regular weekly meeting of the state legislature, Samuel Roberts arose to address the representatives assembled in the back room of the American Hotel in Sacramento.

No more the Captain Roberts who had led the Society of Regulators in their bloody forays against the Spanish-speaking people in the early days of the gold rush, Samuel Roberts had discarded his military uniform and rank. He now wore a rich brocade vest, striped trousers, and velvet-edged cutaway jacket. He had become paunchy from the soft life of a successful gambler. His long nose and lantern jaw were less prominent now that his face had rounded out with good living, but his cold and calculating eyes, and the thin hard line of his mouth, revealed the brutal nature behind that carefully barbered and dapper appearance.

The storekeeper from French Flat was there with him, as a witness, to give testimony of how he had escaped the besieged town.

"Gentlemen," began Roberts in his cockney accent, "it is time we rid this land of that murdering bandit, Murrieta."

The legislators seemed indifferent. This was only one more problem among the many problems of the emerging state.

"Roberts . . . Roberts?" said one of the legislators, a man from San Francisco, who had been there in the early days as the original adobe Mexican outpost of *Yerba Buena*, the northernmost terminal of *el Camino Real*, the Royal Road, developed into the major port of entry for the gold fields.

"Aren't you the Captain Roberts who was the leader of the Hounds?"

Samuel Roberts conceded that he was and the legislators began to talk among themselves, recalling the atrocities and violence committed by the Society of Regulators, generally called the Hounds, in those early days of San Francisco.

To change the subject, Roberts quickly introduced the storekeeper who told how the town of French Flat, and his store, had been taken over by Murrieta.

Uncomfortable, stammering, the storekeeper told how the band had ridden into French Flat.

"An' this one they call Murrieta, he tied them Chinamen together by their queues an' that three-fingered one cut their throats, he did."

"Bravo!" cried one of the legislators. "It's a vile and dastardly thing, this business of importing innocent little children for the foul and contemptible purpose of prostitution. I propose—"

"An' then they killed the barkeep, an' they took over my store, an' collected all the gold everybody had, an' drove us all out of town. They said they'd kill us right there if we didn't leave everything. I had only the clothes on my back. I had a couple thousand dollars in

145

inventory. I could have sold those supplies to the miners for maybe ten or twelve thousand dollars, an' I had to leave it all there. Me an' the missus had to walk all the way. Every penny I had was in that store.''

Poor man, he was so broken up he couldn't continue. Samuel Roberts led him to a chair and turned to face the legislators.

"Your Honor," he addressed the governor, who sat at the head of the table, "if you'll give me the men, I could wipe out those bandits and restore that town to its rightful owners."

"You mean you'd capture them, or drive them out?" asked one of the legislators.

"I mean, with enough men, I'll surround the town. I'll bottle them up and kill every one, including their leader, Murrieta."

"But they let these people go," said another of the legislators. "And as for killing those Chinese pimps, I feel Murrieta did us a service in removing those vice lords. But as for slaughtering Mexican citizens without a trial—"

Gambler that he was, Samuel Roberts realized he had overplayed his hand in revealing his full intention. "But Murrieta killed the bartender, an American citizen," he argued. "He stole the gold which belonged to American citizens."

The governor stilled him by motioning him to be seated while the legislators talked it over. Roberts moved back and sat beside the storekeeper.

After considering the pros and cons, and taking a vote, the legislature decided to oppose the use of militia to secure the town, but voted to post a one-thousand-dollar reward for the capture of Murrieta himself, dead or alive.

As the legislators concluded the meeting and left, the governor remained at the table and motioned to Roberts.

"Sit down, Mr. Roberts."

Roberts moved to a chair beside the governor.

The governor did not turn to look at him but, in the empty room, he lowered his voice to a whisper and spoke to his hands folded on the table before him.

"I'll give you a dozen men for two days. What you do with them is your own business. I do not want to know what happens." He paused, frowning at his folded hands. "But you may be able to collect that reward."

As Roberts started to answer, the governor held up a hand to silence him. He stood, and Roberts stood up, also.

The governor extended his hand, saying, in his full, booming voice, "Nice to have met you, sir. Always glad to meet a constituent of mine."

They shook hands and the governor left the room.

Leading a line of twelve riders, all men of the militia dressed in civilian clothes and fully armed, Samuel Roberts raised one hand as he reined his mount to a stop where the deep woods bordering the trail along the South Fork of the American River opened into a clearing outside of French Flat.

There was no sign of activity on the river, nor in any of the six or seven buildings fronting the main street. A few men could be seen sprawled in front of the saloon, sleeping under their big sombreros. Their attire marked them as Mexicans.

Roberts signaled for silence. He dismounted, walked down the center of the street, and back to his command. In whispers he ordered the men to dismount, then gave orders for the attack.

"It's them," he said. "They're all sleeping off a drunk. Now we'll take no prisoners—men or women. Understand?"

One of the militiamen started to protest. "Not the women—"

Roberts silenced him. "They're *all* outlaws." His voice was hard, commanding. "This is an execution . . . ordered by the governor. We take no prisoners. Understand?"

The men glanced at one another and shrugged—they had been well trained to follow orders—and began to ready their sidearms.

Roberts stopped them. "Keep it as quiet as possible. Use your knives. That way none will be alerted to escape."

The men nodded. They reholstered their guns and drew knives. Quietly, they followed their leader down the main street into the center of French Flat. On a signal from Roberts, they began their mop-up operation.

It was complete and thorough. Most of the outlaw band, sleeping off the effects of that sad parting with their leader, Murrieta, never knew what happened. Before they came fully awake, they were dead. The last few, alerted by a woman's dying scream, had to be shot down as they attempted to escape, but not one of the band survived.

Although Murrieta was missing and no reward could be claimed, Roberts was elated with the success of his mission. For the militiamen, it must be reported that some of them felt a qualm, a moral scruple, until it was discovered that each of the victims had three hundred dollars in gold coin in their pockets.

The days were fair and pleasant at Hornitos. The women reemerged in female attire and makeup, and occupied themselves with womanly activities: housekeeping, cooking, sewing and lace-making, conceiving and bearing children. The men worked at their special skills and in their leisure gathered in the Fandango house to talk and drink and play cards.

The constant alertness of the outlaw trail, the deadly game of kill or be killed, the endless moving on, were quickly forgotten. But one thing would never be forgotten; these were the tried and true, these were the blood-loyal followers of Murrieta, the Avenger. These were family whether related by blood or not.

One golden day in September, after a morning of breaking and training wild horses, after an abundant midday meal, and after a two-hour *siesta*, Joaquín and Three-Fingered Jack sat in the Fandango house playing three-card monte. Claudio was missing because he had gone to Merced the day before.

An alarming, rapid drumming of hoofbeats and a voice calling, "Joaquín! Joaquín!" broke the drowsy afternoon stillness.

Joaquín pushed back his chair. Three-Fingered Jack stood up. Together, they moved toward the entrance. Before they reached it, Claudio burst through the swinging doors.

"Malas noticias!" he cried. "Bad news!"

Staunch man that he was, his eyes were wet and face streaked with tears as he threw his arms about Joaquín, talking incoherently.

"Todo! Todo! They killed them all. The *Americanos!* They slaughtered them!"

Joaquín pressed him back at arm's length. "Claudio! What is this you say? Who is killed? Who killed them?"

Another horse reared to a halt outside the Fandango house and a tall figure pushed through the doors. It was Father Cordova of the mission at Merced. His face was hard, his eyes sad, as he took a folded newspaper from a pocket of his ankle-length habit and offered it to Joaquín.

Joaquín pushed the paper back at the priest. "I cannot read this," he said. He shook his distraught twin cousin. "Claudio! What is it? What's happened?"

Claudio sniffed back tears. He indicated the priest with a wave of his hand. "I brought him to read it to you. Read it, *Padre*."

The Fandango house was filling up. The members of the band and the other residents of Hornitos, drawn by the urgency of the calls and hoofbeats, crowded into the room. Fear, a premonition of something wrong, kept their voices to whispers. Antonia had pushed through the crowd to stand beside Joaquín.

"Well, read it, *Padre*!" Joaquín demanded.

Father Cordova opened the paper and began to read a front-page headline: BRAVE ENCOUNTER OF UNKNOWN CITIZEN-PATRIOTS, LED BY SAMUEL ROBERTS, WITH THE FOLLOWERS OF MURRI-ETA. ENTIRE OUTLAW BAND EXTERMIN-

ATED. PEACE RESTORED TO GOLD FIELDS.

Father Cordova read slowly, pausing as he struggled to translate some of the words. Then he had to read louder to be heard over the sounds of weeping and wailing which increased as he read.

Save Antonia, there was no woman in the room who was not weeping and most of the men had tears in their eyes. These were family and friends who had been slaughtered at French Flat; sisters, brothers, cousins. Antonia caught Joaquín's hand and squeezed tighter as the story of the massacre was revealed.

Joaquín stared at the priest, dumbstruck. When Father Cordova finished reading, Joaquín staggered back to sit in his chair. Finally, above the sounds of grief, he asked, "When?"

Father Cordova placed the newspaper over the cards on the table. It was the *San Francisco Bulletin* of August 10, 1851.

"This paper is now over a month old. That happened the week before it was published. It must have been at least six weeks ago."

Joaquín looked up at Antonia, who was still holding his hand. "Right after we left," he said vacantly. "*Madre de Dios*, why didn't they come with us?"

That started more wailing and Joaquín glanced at Jack. "Get them out of here," he said. "Sit down, *Padre*."

The priest seated himself. Claudio pulled up a chair. Three-Fingered Jack began to herd the others out of the room. The bartender brought glasses and a bottle to the table.

After Jack had cleared the room, after they all had a drink, Joaquín looked at Antonia and said, "Again, you were right, my dove. Our work is not yet done."

"Not dove. I am not your dove."

Joaquín nodded sadly. "No, that is from so long ago. These past weeks have been like old times. I was forgetting."

"*Buitre*! Vulture! Call me your vulture. Because I shall not rest until I drink the blood of this Captain Roberts."

Joaquín closed his eyes. He squeezed his forehead.

Jack poured another round of drinks. "I will kill him," Jack stated, his voice flat, unemotional. "Leave him to me. I will kill Roberts at the very gambling table where he plays."

Joaquín took his hand from his forehead. Would there never be peace? Never an end to violence, a time when the killing would end, when vengeance would be accomplished? The keening sound of the mourners was in his ears; the wailing women, in the plaza outside, grieving lost brothers and sisters, could not be consoled.

Across from him, at the table, the somber figure of the priest in mourning black, a man familiar with death and sorrow, but who spoke of love and mercy and forgiveness. But a man who never saw his woman, more dear than life, ravished and brutalized by the *Americanos*. Beside him, Antonia—*la paloma*, not *el buitre*—met his eyes with an icy, unrelenting stare that made the burden of his guilt unbearable.

Joaquín exhaled. He was committed. By God, or the devil, this man, Samuel Roberts, and he were bound in life as they would be in death, and in the life hereafter.

Turning to Three-Fingered Jack, who would relieve him of this commitment, Joaquín said, "No, I must kill

152

him myself. Not until I kill this man—for myself, for my Antonia, for all these people, my compatriots—will I be at peace.''

He added, ''But not in the city, where he lives. Too many would recognize me.''

He pointed at the newspaper, to a picture which accompanied the headline. It was an artist's drawing, captioned: MURRIETA STILL AT LARGE. It was a close resemblance, but there were dots and splotches in the poor reproduction of the woodcut that looked like freckles. It could have been Joaquín, or his cousin, Claudio.

''If I were recognized I could be killed or captured before I accomplished this deed.''

''I would not be recognized,'' said Three-Fingered Jack.

''But I must kill this Captain Roberts myself,'' said Joaquín. ''Once he escaped me. This time he must die by my own hand.''

''My son—'' began Father Cordova, in his soft voice. ''Did I not tell you, 'Vengeance is mine'?''

Joaquín raised one hand to silence the good priest. ''*Padre*, would God that I could live in peace. But these people died because of me—because they had followed me to right a wrong. This man, Roberts, is an angel of Satan. Answer me, *Padre*, did not even the gentle Jesus fight the devil all his life?''

''And died for it,'' said the priest.

''And so will I, if I must,'' replied Joaquín. ''But I cannot stop now.''

Father Cordova crossed himself and stood up. ''God knows, you have just cause,'' he said. He touched the cross hanging at his breast with his left hand, raised his right hand over those still seated at the table, and blessed them briefly in Latin.

He opened his eyes, touched Joaquín and Antonia upon their heads, saying, *"Vaya con Dios."* Then he departed.

Chapter 14

The foraging party entered the town at the same time that a deputy sheriff was tacking up a reward poster.

As they came up to the cluster of townspeople gathered to read the poster, Joaquín drew his mount to a halt. He glanced over at Three-Fingered Jack and Claudio in an unspoken order to cover him, and dismounted. The two men of the band, riding the seat of the supply wagon, took up their rifles. Two other men, riding horseback behind the wagon, spread out on the far side of the street.

Joaquín walked toward the group of townspeople, pushed through them, and stood beside the deputy sheriff as he hammered in the last tack.

Joaquín looked at the poster intently, his lips softening in a slight smile as he admired the line-drawing portrait. It was larger than the picture in the newspaper. It was a better likeness of himself. This picture had been drawn by a better artist, or from a better description. The printing read: "Dead or Alive. $1,000.00 REWARD." The smaller type Joaquín could not read, but the meaning was clear and the picture a good resemblance.

He glanced around at the deputy sheriff, who stood uncertainly beside him, hammer in hand. He glanced at the man on his other side, a clerk from the store or telegraph office, who had several pencils sticking out of a pocket of his vest. Behind him the townspeople asked uneasy questions of each other, but could not give a positive answer.

Joaquín could smell fear. These *Americanos* could not answer because they were afraid of what the answer would be. "Brave encounter," the newspaper had called it, as "citizen-patriots" slaughtered sleeping men. Joaquín turned to face the townspeople and saw the fear in their eyes. Here they were more evenly matched; ten or so of the men of this town against his group of seven. But these men were not "citizen-patriots." These *Americanos* wanted no "brave encounter" with Murrieta. So they would not believe it was Murrieta.

Joaquín turned his back on them. He took a pencil from the clerk and wrote across the bottom of the poster: "I will pay $1,000.00 myself to the man who can do it." Then boldly signed it: "J. Murrieta."

He jammed the pencil back into the clerk's vest pocket and turned to face the group; they shrank away from him now that their question was answered. Looking each one of them in the eye, he walked slowly back to his horse, mounted, and signaled for the members of the band to continue the forage.

Joaquín remained as the wagon pulled away and up to the general store, where the men went inside and started loading supplies in the wagon. Three-Fingered Jack stayed beside him.

They watched as the deputy sheriff rushed inside the

sheriff's office and came out with another man, wearing a badge.

They watched as the townspeople huddled about the sheriff, imploring him to do nothing.

They heard snatches of words and sentences: "The whole band must be up in the hills somewhere. Let 'em take whatever they want. French Flat. You know what happened there."

The sheriff spoke not one word in reply.

Joaquín and Jack sat their horses, watching the uneasy group of townspeople, until the wagon was loaded. Then, as the wagon returned and passed them, the band moved out, the same as they had come in, keeping their mounts at a slow walk in front of and behind the now loaded wagon.

As Joaquín turned his horse to follow, he waved one hand in a sudden gesture of farewell.

"Yo soy Joaquín."

He spoke the words softly, not as a battle cry, and saw the townspeople cringe and press closer behind their sheriff.

"There it is. The riverboat, *North Star*."

"They're loading the gold."

"Which means it will be departing tomorrow."

"But not with the gold."

"*Es verdad*, we claim that gold for Mexico."

On a promontory overlooking Sacramento, Joaquín and Three-Fingered Jack sat their mounts in waist-high wild oats, dried to a soft beige color, which glowed golden in the October sunlight. Below them, the city, the river, and on the far bank the few buildings of Margaretta lay like a relief map. In the sparkling autumn air, the people and traffic of the streets and the riverfront were plainly visible. Far southward, the buildings of Suttersville could be seen.

The two men sat there quietly, observing the scene.

The riverboat, *North Star*, was berthed at a dock at the northern end of the waterfront. A bank wagon was backed onto the dock and, while the driver and an armed guard sat on a high seat at the front of the wagon, four men unloaded and pushed wheelbarrows of boxed and bagged gold up the gangplank and into the cabin of the boat.

Aboard the boat, the captain and two armed guards watched the loading from the wheelhouse deck.

"You and Claudio will take care of the guards," said Joaquín. "Hold the captain and crew as hostages up on that top deck, where all can see you. Then bring the captain with you when you leave. He will be our safe conduct out of town."

Calmly chewing an oat straw as he watched the scene below, Three-Fingered Jack nodded agreement.

"*Bueno!* We have seen enough, no?"

Jack nodded again and the two men turned their mounts and moved slowly over the crest of the hill.

It was black night, the hour before dawn. Joaquín and his band waited outside the city. From the direction of the docks, a lantern flashed on and off two times. It was a signal that meant the guards and crew of the riverboat, *North Star*, had been secured. Silently, in the darkness, the band moved onto the main street of Sacramento.

Two supply wagons were backed onto the dock where the *North Star* was berthed. Men went aboard to carry the gold from ship to wagons, while others cordoned off the dock and main street. Joaquín stayed with the men guarding the street to ward off any possible attack. On the wheelhouse deck, Claudio and Jack held the captain and crew, gagged and bound hand and foot, except for the captain, whose feet were not tied.

One wagon had been loaded and driven off the dock as dawn flushed the sky. As the twilight of the new day increased, far down on Sutter Street, an early rising shopkeeper came out to sweep his sidewalk. He saw the array of armed, mounted men and dropped his broom and started toward the center of town, glancing back as he hurried on.

One of the band started after him. Joaquín ordered him back.

"Let him go. To stop him would only alert others."

It was full daylight. The second wagon was almost loaded with the last of the gold, when a group of townspeople appeared far down Sutter Street in the center of the town. It was a group of ten or twelve who assembled, then marched toward the mounted band. As they drew closer, it could be seen they were businessmen or merchants, led by an armed man with a sheriff's star on his chest and his armed deputy.

Joaquín gave quiet orders to his band not to shoot as he glanced from the approaching men to the loading of the last wagon. He moved his horse to the center of the street, in front of the band, and the group of townspeople stopped, huddled behind the sheriff and his deputy.

The deputy drew his gun. The sheriff slapped it down.

"Put that damn thing away!"

A short man, dressed in a business suit and top hat, pulled at the sheriff's arm. "Do something! Stop 'em!"

The sheriff shook his arm free. "You be quiet, Ephraim."

"But that's my gold they're stealing!"

The sheriff turned to look at him. "I know that," he said quietly.

"Well, do something!"

"What do you expect me to do, die for it?"

"Stop them! Arrest them! They're stealing my gold!"

The sheriff looked around at the others in the group. "Any of you want to die for that gold?"

The little man in the top hat became frantic. "Stop 'em! We gotta stop 'em!" he yelled at the others. "He's the sheriff. Make him do something!"

The others moved uneasily. One of them said, "Ah, shut up, Ephraim. You want to get us all killed?"

The little man went crazy. He yanked the gun from the sheriff's holster. The sheriff tried to grab it, but the man darted away. Holding the gun in both hands, at shoulder level, he turned to face the mounted men of the band.

Back in the center of town a larger group was gathering. Disorganized, uncertain of what was happening, they talked and pointed but remained far down the street.

Simultaneously watching the crowd down the street, the activity on the *North Star*, and the group in front of him, Joaquín addressed the businessman with the gun.

"*Señor*," he said calmly, "the gold is not worth your life."

He sat relaxed in the saddle. One hand held the reins of his horse as he pointed to the deputy with his free hand. "And you, Deputy," he said, smiling, "throw away your gun."

From the side of his eye, he saw Three-Fingered Jack and Claudio leave the *North Star* with the ship's captain walking before them, saw them mount up. The men loading the wagon had finished and climbed into the wagon bed. Down the street the crowd, led by a man in a militia uniform, started toward them.

"Deputy, your gun," repeated Joaquín.

"Do what he says," snapped the sheriff and the deputy tossed his gun aside.

The second and last wagon was moving off the dock, into the street, and away. Jack, with the ship's captain riding in front of him on the saddle, moved up beside Joaquín. Jack had his pistol at the captain's ear.

Joaquín smiled disarmingly at the little businessman. *"Señor . . ."*

The man was holding the gun in both hands, at arm's length, clenching the grip so tight it trembled. Now he pointed it at Joaquín.

"Ephraim!" cried the sheriff. "Don't be a damn fool. You want to get us all killed!"

"They're stealing my gold!"

"To hell with the gold!"

"It's my gold! Mine! Mine!"

"Can't you see they got the captain?" argued the sheriff. "They'll kill him and us, too!"

"Not before I kill him!"

It was time to leave. The crowd coming up Sutter Street had increased and was getting within pistol range.

"*Señor*," Joaquín repeated, extending his free hand in a pleading gesture. "Give me the gun."

The little man was beyond reason. His eyes were wild. The gun shook uncontrollably in his two clenched fists.

Joaquín waved his hand suddenly to distract the man, dug with his spurs and, as the horse reared up, the little man staggered back a step and fired his shot wild. As his horse came down, Joaquín drew his pistol and shot the little man in the forehead.

He wheeled his horse, yelling, "*Vamos!*" and the band wheeled with him, galloping to catch up with the wagons.

Chapter 15

Burgoyne's Bank was on Montgomery Street. It was a brick building with a fireproof basement, erected at enormous outlay after the original bank building burned to the ground in the fire which swept San Francisco in the summer of 1851.

The bank manager came hurrying from his office as Joaquín turned from the teller's cage, folding a small piece of paper, which he tucked into his vest pocket. As Joaquín crossed the lobby to where Antonia was seated, waiting for him to conclude this business, the manager caught up with him.

"Mr. Carillo," said the manager, a whispy, clerkish type of man, wearing pince-nez eyeglasses, "I welcome you as a depositor in our bank. Any way we can be of service . . ."

Joaquín crooked his arm as Antonia arose and she placed her hand through his arm. She wore a big, ostrich-plumed hat and pinched waist gown and white satin gloves.

The manager bowed slightly, saying, "Madam," then corrected himself. *"Señora."*

Antonia nodded and smiled.

"Good day, sir," said Joaquín and jammed his derby hat on as they started for the door. The stiff hat was uncomfortable, but he wore it now as part of his businessman costume.

As the manager started back to his office, the teller handed him a duplicate of the paper Joaquín had tucked in his vest pocket. It was a bank draft for a deposit of forty thousand dollars. The manager took off his glasses to stare wide-eyed at the teller.

"What was it—coin or raw gold?" he asked.

"It was bullion."

"You had it assayed?"

"Yes, sir. The assay office stamped it 99 percent pure."

"Then I see nothing wrong in the transaction."

"No, sir," said the teller. "Only how would a greaser get that kind of a fortune? And why's he sending it to Sonora?"

"Johnson," intoned the manager, removing his pince-nez to pronounce a business dictum, "we do not refer to those who bring us their custom as greasers. Nor as spics, or chinks, or *chilenos*. The banking business knows neither race nor nationality. You see, gold is universal."

"Yes, sir," murmured the teller. "I'll remember that." And he went back to his high stool.

They were seated at a table in the elegant dining room of the Parker House on the Plaza in San Francisco.

Antonia was dressed in the latest fashion, with a bustle and puffed sleeves, in a gown that had been shipped from New York City. On her feet were dainty,

164

over-the-ankle, white-kid, high-button shoes. On her hands were white lace gloves from Belgium. Jewels which flashed fire at her ears and throat reflected the light of kerosene chandeliers.

Joaquín, dressed in his business suit, wore a gray satin cravat with a diamond stickpin.

The gambler, William Burns, was with them.

The table was laid with Irish linen, silver, Chinese porcelain, and crystal stemware. They were eating oysters, served in the half-shell on Majolica plates.

At one end of the high-ceilinged, brightly lighted room a string quartet made delicate sounds. At the other end of the room was the bar, for men only, partitioned off with an arbor through which one could see the array of bottles, sparkling glassware, and the huge reclining-nude oil painting over the center of the bar.

A waiter in formal dress hovered beside their table to turn a bottle, bedded in ice, in a silver bucket. As they finished and the oyster dishes were removed, the waiter popped the cork and poured champagne.

Joaquín tasted the sparkling liquid and wrinkled his nose. "I am so used to tequila that I cannot say if this is good or bad."

Will Burns tasted of his glass, smiled, and closed his eyes in appreciation. "Superb," he said, touching thumb to forefinger.

Antonia sipped. "It has not much fire." Then she swallowed the glassful in one gulp.

Burns was horrified. "No! No! It should be savored."

Antonia laughed. "You savor it. I will drink it up." Her eyes sparkled in the bright light of the chandeliers. Her laughter was like music. In this room of fashionably dressed women, her slim, dark beauty was outstanding.

She drank her second glass of champagne slower. "I think I like this life in the big city." She smiled coquettishly at Joaquín. "You must take me out dining more often."

The first course, filleted sturgeon with a mornay sauce sprinkled with paprika, had been served when a man on his way to the bar passed their table, stopped, and turned to look at them.

It was Samuel Roberts.

A dandy, in his chalk-striped trousers, velveteen vest, broadcloth tailcoat, and French-heeled boots, he stared at them, uncertain, but frozen in an attitude of surprised awareness. He flexed his soft white hands, hands that were lightning quick at cutting and dealing, or on the trigger of a derringer.

Joaquín slowly arose. His icy stare riveted on this hated enemy. Unconsciously, one hand slid inside his coat and the two men stood in silence for a long moment.

Joaquín's mind was racing. Instinct told him to draw and kill the man here and now. Reason held him back. He could not escape, with Antonia, through the crowds of people. He could not escape without her, because she would be questioned and held and jailed as a member of the outlaw band.

At the bar all the men were in business suits or evening clothes. They talked quietly of business affairs or politics as they stood before the polished mahogany bar. The air was blue with cigar smoke. One man, wearing a Stetson hat and range clothes, looked out of place. His voice was loud as he jostled those nearest him, trying to engage the gentlemen in conversation. Discouraged, he turned his back on the bar and looked out through the entrance in the arbor to the dining room.

The quiet elegance of the scene was in sharp contrast to this stranger's dress and manners. Then he saw the two men standing at one of the tables and recognized one of them. Drink in hand, he moved toward the arbor entrance to the dining room and called out: "Roberts! Hey Capt'n, yuh ole horned toad. I'm waiting for you!"

In the dining room, all heads turned toward that slurred, drunken sound. All but Joaquín and his hated enemy. Their eyes were still locked. Samuel Roberts moved back a step. Another step backward. Then gambled that he could safely turn his back in this crowded room, and walked on into the bar.

Joaquín watched him walk away. He saw the two men meet at the bar and imprinted the features and form of this acquaintance on his, Joaquín's, mind. Any friend of Roberts was another enemy.

Finally, he sat and unfolded his napkin to resume the meal, but his eyes were still on the two men in the bar, who were now standing in the arbor entrance looking back at their table.

"Will, who is the one wearing the big hat?"

"Name's Harry Love. He arrived today on the packet from Los Angeles."

"Do you know his business? Why he would be here? Why he would be meeting with Captain Roberts?"

Burns shook his head. "I know only that he's a deputy sheriff from Los Angeles."

Antonia's eyes had lost their sparkle. There was a cold glitter in them now, as she said, "This is no good.

Let us leave this place. I feel death here."

"Stay," said Joaquín.

Roberts and Love had moved to the bar and were leaning over it in earnest conversation.

Joaquín picked up his silver fork. "It is better that we know our enemies. That we follow them out instead of them following us out," he said, as he turned his attention to the food on the table.

In the month of May, 1853, the state legislature, sitting in the town of Benicia, across the bay from San Francisco, listened attentively as Samuel Roberts introduced the former deputy sheriff of Los Angeles as the man to rid California of the bandit, Murrieta.

With an unanimous vote, the governor, John Bigler, offered a reward of five thousand dollars for Joaquín Murrieta, dead or alive, and lesser amounts for others of the outlaw band. Also, the legislature passed a bill authorizing the formation of a company of California Rangers to be led by Captain Harry Love, for the sole purpose of ridding the state of California of its outlaws.

Twenty men were enlisted for a period of ninety days at a salary of one hundred and fifty dollars a month. By the first of June, after a grueling training period, Captain Love and his twenty Rangers were ready to begin the pursuit of Murrieta and his band.

Captain Love had dedicated himself, and his men, to the success of this hunt. They would not return without the bandit or proof of his death.

PART III

Chapter 16

Claudio Carillo was galloping along the trail that led to Hornitos. His handsome young face, burned so brown by wind and sun that his freckles were not now apparent, showed signs of strain and apprehension. His horse was lathered and blowing, exhausted by the long run from Merced.

At the first lookout station west of the town, Claudio slowed his mount to a walk and leaned forward to rub its neck. Although there was nothing to be seen, he waved to the concealed lookout. Almost there, he let the horse choose its own gait. There had been other lookouts farther back. He knew the news of his arrival was already known in Hornitos.

To his left the creek sparkled sunlight through the trees. On his right was a densely wooded hillside. In a moment he caught flashes of the clearing ahead and the buildings of the town.

Hornitos was a growing place. There were now adobe houses along the trail leading to the town, and the plaza was completely surrounded by stores, gambling houses, *cantinas*, and rooming houses, since there was no hotel. The main building on the plaza was the

Fandango house, where the members of the outlaw band gathered. Across from it, the jail was in the exact center of the town. Behind the jail, on the slope of the hill, was the cemetery and, west of that, the brewery which was fitted as a fortress with loopholes on all four sides.

This was Joaquín Murrieta's hideout. All Spanish-speaking, the residents of Hornitos were either members of the band, or friendly to them. Here, they could withstand an army from the provisioned and fortified brewery, or flee through a trapdoor in the floor of the Fandango house, by tunnel, to the riverbank where horses were always tethered.

As his tired mount approached the plaza, Claudio dismounted and gave the reins to a boy, giving instructions to care for the animal. Members of the gang welcomed him from the veranda of the Fandango house.

Inside, everything stopped as he moved toward the table where Joaquín sat dealing monte. Joaquín's face hardened as he listened to this latest news from the outside world.

"California Rangers?" said Joaquín. "Who says this?"

"It's in all the newspapers," said Claudio. "They are led by a man named Harry Love."

"Love?" Joaquín repeated. Then remembered. "*Sí*, this is the one I saw with Captain Roberts."

"*Sí*. And Captain Roberts rides with him."

At the sound of that hated name, Joaquín slammed his cards on the table, jumped up, and began to pace the room. "This man! I will never be free of him until I kill him," he muttered grimly.

172

"*Sí*. You will have to kill him," agreed Claudio. "You will have to kill all of these Rangers . . . or they will kill you. They will kill all of us."

Claudio continued slowly, trying to remember the exact words as Father Cordova had read them to him from the newspaper. "The governor has authorized these California Rangers to rid California of its bandits."

"Then I will kill them all!" said Joaquín.

"There are twenty of them."

Joaquín cocked his head on one side and strutted back to face his twin cousin, who looked so much like him. "So I will kill all twenty of them!" He flung out one hand in a reckless gesture. *"Yo soy Joaquín!"*

At that, the men in the room shouted loud cheers. They all began to talk at once as they resumed drinking, bragging of past conquests, and plotting this coming battle.

Claudio had more to say. He shook his head sadly as he repeated what Father Cordova had told him.

"No matter how many of these Rangers we kill, they will recruit more men and train them. Joaquín, they will not stop until we are wiped out. All dead, or escaped back to Mexico."

Law and order had come to California by the year 1853.

Before that, a gambling dispute was quickly settled by an exchange of gunfire, a body would be carried outside, and the game would be resumed. Now the militia was called in. The names of witnesses were taken. The surviving participant was then held in jail for trial, to be judged by a jury of peers and sentenced by a circuit judge, who held court at monthly intervals.

Usually it was the gambler, his soft white hands as quick with gun or knife as they were with the cards, who was the survivor held for court. And so it was that William Burns was awaiting trial in the jail on Commercial Street in San Francisco.

After four days in these unsanitary conditions, unshaven, sick of the smell of urine, his clothes soiled and stinking of perspiration and filth, his stomach empty and growling with hunger, the gambler, Burns, was surprised to be visited by Samuel Roberts and Captain Harry Love of the newly organized California Rangers.

As the cell door opened and the two men came in, Burns arose from the sagging cot where he had been brooding.

"What are you doing here?" he asked bluntly.

Roberts smiled expansively. He wore stylish, immaculate, pressed clothing. He was barbered and manicured and smelled of bay rum. "We're in the same profession," he said, as if that mattered. "I thought I could be of some help to you."

In comparison, Burns felt doubly filthy. Suspicion tugged at him. He glanced at the deputy sheriff from Los Angeles who was leaning casually against the bars of the cell door, then looked back at the former leader of the Society of Regulators. His mind went back to the hanging on Telegraph Hill and the carnage at Clark's Point, both executed by the Society of Regulators.

"Why would you help me? I've never been your friend."

Roberts glanced about the squalid cell. "I'm sure you'd be glad to get out of here." He pinched his nose and breathed through his mouth, as he said, "If only for a breath of fresh air." Then he added, "And a hot bath—wouldn't that feel good? A change of clothes. A good meal. A decent bed."

Suspicion gave way to impatience. "What are you getting at? What do you want?"

Roberts spread his soft white hands. "A little help from you in return. That's not too much to ask, is it?"

Burns waited. He knew there was more.

Roberts pointed to Love. "Do you know the captain of the California Rangers?"

"I know of him."

"And you know that he's been appointed by the governor to rid California of its outlaws."

"You mean Murrieta."

Roberts nodded. "And you know Murrieta."

"Yes, I know him. But I'd never betray him."

"Did I say 'betray'?"

"No," said Burns, "but if that's what you mean—you can deal me out."

Harry Love stepped forward. He took off his Army-issue hat, which all of the Rangers now wore, and wiped the sweatband with a dirty rag that served as handkerchief.

"Mr. Burns," he stated with clipped military precision, "I want you only to identify this man. I don't know him. I saw him once, from a distance, when I had a few drinks too many. None of my men know him, except Roberts, here. On a dangerous mission such as this, one man to identify the quarry is not enough."

"And you want me to point him out before you kill him," said Burns. "A Judas!"

"I want to know that I get the man I'm after and not some innocent stranger."

175

"You mean the right man so you'll be sure to get the reward. It's up to five thousand dollars now, isn't it?" William Burns moved to the cell door and opened it. Waving one hand toward the corridor, he said, "Get out!"

Roberts chuckled. "I thought you'd be difficult," he said. He sat on the edge of the filthy cot and lit a cigar, his long horse face and lantern jaw losing its fullness as he sucked on the match flame.

"That's why I saw your attorney before we came here." He blew the fragrance of the cigar smoke toward Burns. "He has little hope for you. The two witnesses say the man you killed was unarmed." He paused to puff on the cigar luxuriously. "And they say that you provoked the incident by cheating the man out of his entire earnings in the gold fields."

"It's a lie! He lost fairly, then called me a cheat."

Roberts spread his soft white hands. "That's what I thought." He smiled smugly and blew another cloud of smoke into the fetid air of the cell. "In fact, I was there and could be a witness that you did not cheat. I even have the gun the miner had concealed in his belt."

He nodded seriously at the astounded Burns. "And I have friends in the governor's office. This matter never need come to trial. I could have you out of here tomorrow, with a decree signed by the governor himself."

The gambler, Burns, released his hold on the jail-cell door and walked slowly back to sit on the edge of the filthy cot beside Samuel Roberts. Two gamblers, in a new game, with the life of Murrieta at stake.

Finally, Burns spoke. "All right. I'll identify Murrieta for you."

Roberts smiled triumphantly. "I thought you

would." He stood and, taking a cigar from his breast pocket, offered it to the crestfallen loser. "Here, try one of my cigars. It'll make the air smell sweeter."

Together, the two visitors left, leaving the cell door standing open. It was a few minutes before the guard came to close and lock the door and, by that time, Burns had crumpled the expensive cigar in his balled fist and slammed the shreds of tobacco on the cell floor.

The Fandango house in Hornitos was serving as a meeting hall for the band. There was an unusual air of solemnity about the men and women gathered there. They watched silently as Joaquín moved to the bar and turned to face them.

"*Compadres*, it is time for us to break up. I want you all to go home and live in peace with your families and friends."

Suddenly, they all began talking to each other and there were scattered voices raised in opposition.

"*Amigos*, I cannot ask more of you. Long and faithfully you have served me and our cause. But now these California Rangers are too great a threat. No matter how many we kill, there will always be more to pursue us. Instead of being the hunters, we will be the hunted. Anyhow, our work is done. We cannot fight an army. It is now up to Mexico to supply trained troops if this land is ever to be reclaimed."

As the men and women discussed this, Joaquín continued. "There is much gold and many horses. I want you to take it all back to Mexico with you. It is yours. Divide it. Live in peace."

There were general cries of approval, but Joaquín silenced them. He had more to say.

"I do not go with you because there is still one thing more to be done—to kill Captain Roberts—and this I must do myself."

Suddenly, there was movement. Antonia stood up and started toward him. As she came before him at the bar, he grasped her arm and held her with his eyes.

"Quiet!" he said softly. "I am their leader. I want no one to oppose me."

Then putting his arm about her waist, he said to the room, "I want you to leave at sunup. Travel as a group so you will be safe from attack. And *vaya con Dios*."

The men whooped and hollered. The women wept. They all began talking and drinking, but Three-Fingered Jack and Claudio went to each table to hurry them along, to pack and prepare for the long journey.

Joaquín stayed at the bar, his arm about Antonia's waist, as he waved and spoke to the members of his band as they left. He smiled at Antonia, and Antonia smiled with him at the departing men and women, but he held her wrist in a steely grip to keep her silent.

As the room cleared, Joaquín released his hold on Antonia and grinned at her angry expression. "I know," he said, "you do not take orders like the rest of my company."

"I stay with you."

"I want you with me."

"If you do not kill him, I will."

"You will do as I say. This is too dangerous now that these Rangers are organized."

"Danger?" Her tone was contemptuous. "I care not for danger."

"But I do."

Joaquín took her hands in his, gently this time,

saying, "I care very much for your safety, *cara mia*. When this is over, when my vow is fulfilled, when Captain Roberts has paid with his life for all he has done, I want us to go home also. To build a life together. To raise many sons. And the finest of my golden horses."

Antonia looked away from his tender, pleading eyes. In her heart, an old dream rekindled. Joaquín took advantage of the moment.

"For now, I want you to go to Monterey. There you will be safe and you can learn more about these Rangers and whatever moves they plan to make. Claudio will go with you and bring back to me whatever information you feel is important."

Antonia nodded.

"And when my work is done, I will send for you."

Antonia responded by putting her arms about him and hugging him tight. She pressed her head to his breast and deep inside her, the young bride, Rosita Felix, stirred. The old dreams reawakened from when they were first married and life held so much promise and joy. So long ago, it seemed. So cold, those dreams. So faint, the hope they ever could again be realized. But hope stirred. Faith revived as she held Joaquín tightly to her, this man she had loved from earliest childhood.

Back at the table where they had been sitting before this final meeting of the band, others now sat, talking and drinking and bragging in boastful tones. These, too, would not take orders like the rest of the band. These would stay with Murrieta to the end.

Three-Fingered Jack and Claudio Carillo would never leave him. The others who would not go home without Joaquín were: Luis Vulvia, Pedro Gonzales, Manuel Sevalio, Fernando Fuentes, José Ochovo, Florencio Cruz, Rafael Quintano; names now scarcely remembered in the history of California. But then and there, in 1853, at that table in the Fandango house in Hornitos, these were vital, fearless, trusted, loyal men, all seriously grieved by the *Americanos*, all with their hands stained by *gringo* blood, all ready to die for a leader they loved, and for a cause they knew was just.

Chapter 17

The first move of the California Rangers drew a blank. Their raid on Hornitos was unsuccessful.

The main body of the band had left for Mexico weeks before, taking the gold and a great herd of horses with them. The day before the raid, Claudio Carillo had arrived with a message from Monterey and Joaquín and the men still with him were gone within an hour.

Now, as the Rangers milled about the plaza on tired horses, making a great display of their accoutrements and arms, and squared Army hats, there were only a few residents standing on the verandas or in doorways of the *cantinas*, stores and rooming houses of the deserted town, to be impressed by this military exhibition.

Samuel Roberts and William Burns, dressed in business suits, arrived last and forced their horses through the crowd of Rangers, up to the Fandango house where Captain Harry Love's horse was tethered. They dismounted and, while Burns rubbed aching muscles, Roberts went inside.

Love was questioning the owner and the girls.

Roberts listened, impatient and disgruntled, for a

while, then went behind the bar, pushed his gun into the owner's belly, and led him out into the center of the room.

"Get a rope," he said to Harry Love.

"What are you doing?"

"You want information, don't you?"

"Yes, but—"

"I'll get it for you or we'll string this greaser up. And every other greaser in the town, until we get the information we want. I know how to deal with these people."

Harry Love's eyes narrowed. He looked about the room. The girls were huddled at the far end of the bar. Two old men sat at one table. William Burns stood in the doorway.

Love unsnapped the flap of his military holster. He moved toward Roberts.

"Turn him loose," he said.

"No, that's not the way. You want information. He'll give it to us or we'll hang him. That's the only way you'll get it."

Love moved closer. His eyes bored into Roberts'.

"Turn him loose, I said."

Roberts backed up a step, still holding his gun on the trembling Mexican. "You're all wrong. That's not the way to deal with these people."

Love had moved up beside the Fandango house owner. He shoved the man out of the way while his other hand hovered at his holstered gun, but his eyes never left Roberts'.

"You'll give no orders in my command," he said evenly. "Now put your gun down. And get out of here."

Roberts swallowed hard. He rammed his gun into its holster and glanced away from Love's boring eyes.

"They're all bandits," he said. "Every one of them should be killed or driven out of California."

"Get out," said Love, nodding to the doorway.

Roberts stood there, angry and defiant, the gambler in him figuring the odds.

Love continued, "We're not out to harm innocent nationals, but to capture, or kill, Murrieta and his band. Nobody else."

Roberts stood his ground and glared at him. And figured the odds were too great.

Captain Love had more to say. "While you ride with me, you follow my orders or I'll shoot you down right here." Their eyes locked. Breathing was suspended as fingers inched toward gun butts and time stood still. Until Roberts looked away.

"Now, GET OUT!"

Roberts recoiled as if he had been struck. He started toward the swinging doors and saw Burns turn and move through them, a witness to his defeat.

Outside, in the brilliant sunlight of the plaza, the Rangers had quieted their horses. Still mounted, they awaited the appearance and next command of their captain.

Joaquín got his first sight of the California Rangers from a high place in the Santa Cruz mountains, the range which parallels the coast between Santa Cruz and San José.

He and the ones who would not leave him had been out of Hornitos ten days, and raided San José for food and ammunition. Instead of heading back into the Sierra Nevada mountains, they moved toward Monterey, the headquarters of the Rangers. Knowing the news of the raid would reach Love, they camped above a pass in the mountains on the old Spanish trail from Santa Cruz to San José, and waited.

The next day, the Rangers headed for the scene of the raid. From their hiding place, high above the pass, Joaquín and his men watched the Rangers ride down the road at a gallop, strung out over half a mile, in single file, with their captain in the lead. Farther back, Roberts and Burns trailed the Rangers, showing signs of the strain of this unaccustomed life on the trail.

From this vantage point they could have killed some of the Rangers, but Joaquín had ordered no shooting. He wanted only to observe them. He noted with approval, as one commander would admire the good tactics of his opponent, that Love signaled the riders to a walk once they were through the danger of the narrow pass, and realized that these men were well trained. Love's Rangers were men capable of surviving in any terrain, they followed orders, were good horsemen, and probably skilled marksmen.

Battle plans formed in Joaquín's mind. He would have to lure them into a longer pass and have his men spaced over a wider area. "What is our friend, Will Burns, doing with them?" he wondered aloud.

Three-Fingered Jack, who lay beside Joaquín as they looked over the rim of the cliff, could not answer that one. Nor could any of the others.

It was the end of June. Ocean breezes cooled their camp high above the pass at midday, and, at night, the stars hung immense and close in a velvet sky.

Joaquín had found a retreat route that would lead them quickly to the San Joaquín valley and the Sierra Nevadas beyond, so they stayed encamped above the pass, with only one lookout at the San José end. Their food supply had been replenished. They knew the location of the enemy. They waited.

"The Rangers! They're coming back!" It was the lookout, scrambling over rocks as he gave the alarm.

The lounging men took their time getting up and checking their arms. Their saddled horses stood quietly picketed.

"Only one volley. Then we ride," said Joaquín to the men as they moved into position, lying prone, at the rim of the pass.

As the Rangers came within rifle range, they were bunched closer than before. One of the Rangers rode beside Captain Love. Back in the file, a few rode side by side, careless of impending danger. As they came directly below on the old Spanish trail, Joaquín stood, revealing himself, and shouted: *"Yo soy Joaquín!"*

As the Rangers looked up, the gang opened fire.

Horses fell. Riders milled about, seeking cover. Some men fell or were thrown from their mounts.

"Got 'em, *por Dios*!" cried Joaquín, gleeful and carefree as a boy. *"Vamos!"* Running to the picket line, he vaulted into the saddle and put spurs to his horse.

Behind him, the others of the gang followed their leader at a breakneck gallop.

As the bells of the church in Monterey tolled, calling the faithful to evening vespers, the plaza in front of the ancient mission filled with leisurely strolling *señoritas*, in black lace and irridescent satin, hiding their nervous giggles and titters behind half-spread fans. Gay *caballeros*, dashing in tight velvet jackets, braved the suspicious glances of watchful *señoras*, chaperoning the girls on their way to church, in their attempts to catch the attention of a particular young lady.

Antonia moved into the evening promenade unnoticed. She wore a long gown over breeches and boots, her trail clothes which she wore constantly, ready to ride at a moment's notice. On her head she wore a lace mantilla to hide her shorn hair.

As the good *padre* opened the doors and came out to welcome his parishioners, the bells stopped ringing. A stillness swept the plaza. All conversation stopped.

A file of riders, coming from the north, had entered the far end of the main street of Monterey and were making a slow and somber progress toward the plaza. Two of the horses carried dead men draped over the saddle, with head and hands hanging limp on one side and booted feet hanging down the other.

Captain Love led the procession into the plaza and stopped his horse in front of the livery stable. There, he raised one hand in a signal for the Rangers to dismount.

Soft orders were given. The two bodies were lifted from the saddles and carried into the barber shop; the barber was also the undertaker.

The horses were led into the stable and the Rangers waited in a restless group as Love talked to the sheriff.

Antonia crossed the plaza and stood on the boardwalk in front of the general store, close enough to hear what the men said. Samuel Roberts, she knew, was one of the Rangers, but she was shocked to see the gambler,

William Burns, among them. She could only hear mumblings among the men until Love came back to the group.

"There's accommodations at the hotel for all of you," she heard Love say. "We'll ride out in the morning."

"Not me, Captain," said one of the Rangers. "I came out here to hunt gold, not outlaws."

"Me, too," said another. "I won't be ridin' with you in the morning."

They argued briefly and she heard Love say, "This ain't the Army. I can't force you."

Four of the men left the group of Rangers and headed for the saloon. The others followed Love to the hotel. As they passed, William Burns saw Antonia. His glance showed surprise and guilt. He started toward her. She motioned him away.

Roberts came after Burns and caught his arm.

"You ain't cutting out on us, Will." He called over his shoulder to Captain Love. "Hey, Captain, you're losing another recruit."

Burns yanked his arm free and, at the same moment, saw Antonia shrink back against the wall of the general store. Roberts, who was attempting to grab Burns, glanced over and saw Antonia, also. For a moment their eyes met.

Against the wall, Antonia slipped her hand inside the folds of her long gown and grasped the butt of a six-gun tucked in the belt of her breeches. Roberts showed no sign of recognition. All his attention was centered on the gambler, Burns.

As Captain Love came up to them, Roberts said, "This is one who can't leave us, Captain."

Harry Love looked at the two men.

"Well, what is it?" he asked Burns. "You riding with us or do I turn you over to the sheriff, right now?"

Will Burns was straightening his broadcloth coat. Angrily, he brushed dust from the sleeves of it. He glared at Captain Love. "That's not much of a choice, is it?"

"It's the only choice you've got."

"All right, I'm riding with you," said Burns, angry in voice and mien. Then to Samuel Roberts, he said softly, "Roberts, I swear if Murrieta don't kill you, I will."

Roberts laughed nervously. He turned away from Burns' angry countenance and his glance rested for a moment on Antonia again. In the shadows, now, as the twilight deepened, Antonia gripped the gun butt tighter.

Then the three men moved away.

For one hundred and fifty dollars a month, Harry Love had recruited some good men. The twenty were fourteen now, but these remaining were the best, the most dedicated. W. S. Henderson, George Evans, John Nuttall, Bob Masters, Lafayette Black; these are the names handed down in history from official files and old newspaper accounts, men who put their comfort and their lives on the line in the cause of law and order, and one hundred and fifty dollars a month.

W. S. Henderson was the tracker, who followed the trail of Murrieta as the gang rode south on *el Camino Real*, the Royal Road, which paralleled the coast from San Francisco to Loreto in Baja, California. Murrieta

188

went through San Luis Obispo at night. The Rangers followed the next morning. Near Santa Ynez the outlaw band left the *Camino Real* at a rocky place, and the Rangers rode into Santa Barbara before realizing they had lost the trail.

Without pausing, they turned back to pick up the trail at the one spot where Henderson knew it could have been lost. At that rocky place there was only one way to go. Westward was the Pacific Ocean. Eastward lay the Diablo mountain range which lay between the Royal Highway and the San Joaquín valley. The Rangers turned right, riding in spaced single file, so that no ambush attack could get them all.

From a high place, Joaquín saw the Rangers as they entered the chaparral and underbrush of the foothills of the Diablo Mountains. He ordered the seven, who would not leave him, to lead the Rangers on a chase, north, toward Paso Robles. Three-Fingered Jack stayed with Joaquín on the ridge.

From this vantage point, they watched as the Rangers caught sight of a burning ranch building and turned north. Then Jack and Joaquín followed the Rangers, as the Rangers pursued the seven members of the band.

At the burned-out ranch, Love and the Rangers kept going, pressing the pursuit. Samuel Roberts and William Burns stopped to rest.

Only an outbuilding had been burned to attract the Rangers. Joaquín and Jack left their horses in an arroyo and approached, through the underbrush, on foot. They found Roberts and Burns sitting on a bench on the shady side of the house, drinking cool tea and talking to the rancher, his wife, and young son.

With drawn guns, they came around the corner of the house and broke up the tea party.

"*Señor—Señora*, stay back." Joaquín motioned for the ranch owner and his wife to move aside. Jack guided the *gringo* family away from the gamblers.

Joaquín moved closer to the two startled men.

"Will, you are in bad company."

The gambler, Burns, spread his hands, a habitual gesture to show there were no aces up his sleeves. "Not because I want to be here. I was forced into it."

Joaquín nodded, smiling at the gambler who had always been his friend. "I believe you, *amigo*." Then, speaking an order to the two of them, he said, "Your guns. Throw them over here."

Burns set aside his glass of tea and threw his derringer to Joaquín, who caught it in his left hand.

The instant Joaquín caught the derringer, Roberts pulled his gun and would have fired, but Joaquín saw the move and shot the Army Colt out of his hand.

With bloody hand, Roberts leaped up, yelling his outrage, and lunged toward the *gringo* family. Scrabbling on hands and knees, he grabbed the young boy from the mother's hand and held the kid as a shield.

Panting, desperate, he moved the boy toward his Army Colt lying on the ground. The boy struggled to free himself and started to cry. Roberts inched him along. The mother shrieked a plea of mercy, then darted, heedlessly, to her son. In the following melee, Roberts grabbed her as the boy scampered away.

The gun still lay on the ground.

Inching closer to the gun, held powerless in Roberts'

grip, the woman said, "Oh, please . . ." It was like a prayer.

They were beside the gun now. Roberts had only to stoop to retrieve it.

The scene seemed frozen in time. Burns sat rigid on the bench. Jack held the rancher, his gun pressed into the *gringo's* back. Roberts held the woman with her arms pinned behind her, her body thrust forward for his shield. The boy was on hands and knees, where he had fallen, looking up, wide-eyed, at the notorious bandit, Murrieta.

"Oh, please . . ." the woman's voice came again in a faint, pleading whisper.

Joaquín frowned. Then, slowly, he nodded to the brave mother. He turned his gun aside and dropped it in his holster.

Roberts bent to grab the Colt. The woman brought her knee up in a sharp blow to his chin. She fell away, off balance, and Joaquín blew the gambler's head off with the derringer he still held in his left hand.

The mother darted to her son. The father moved toward them and helped his weeping wife to her feet. Joaquín looked at the deadly derringer in his hand. He glanced at the body of Samuel Roberts, the face mutilated beyond recognition. Then glanced over at Burns and hefted the weapon.

"Is a good gun," he said, smiling, and slipped it into his back pocket.

Then he turned to Three-Fingered Jack who still held his revolver at the ready. "Our work is done. *Vamos*."

Jack indicated the *gringo* family with his pistol.

Joaquín shook his head. "No, we have already

caused them enough trouble. That is a brave woman."

As they walked to their horses in the arroyo, he told Jack, "There will be no more killing. Not even these Rangers. They are good men, doing what they think is right. Now that Captain Roberts is dead, we are finished. I want only to get my Antonia and go home to Sonora."

Chapter 18

Antonia was about to retire. She had taken off the long gown she wore over her trail clothes of breeches and shirt, and had slipped off her boots. She was in the bedroom of a two-room adobe house in the Mexican section of Monterey. The family who harbored her—father, mother, and two children—had given up their bed and all slept in the main room which was kitchen, living room, dining room, and now sleeping quarters for them.

Claudio Carillo slept on straw in a shed which housed a goat and chickens. They stayed here, rather than in a hotel, to be less conspicuous.

Antonia was about to blow out the kerosene lamp beside her bed when a light tapping on the door stopped her. It was a signal. In bare feet she crossed the main room, lifted the bar on the door, and opened it.

Claudio brushed past her, with another man right behind.

She replaced the bar and led the two men back into her lighted chamber. There, she saw the other man was Luis Vulvia, one of the faithful who would not leave Joaquín.

She waited. Then said, "You bring news. Is it good, or bad?"

"*Sí. Bueno.* It is good news, *señora*. The Captain Roberts is dead."

Antonia felt a sudden weakness and sat on the side of her bed. All these years, sustained only by a driving need for vengeance, and now it was ended.

"Who? How?" She had to know.

Luis spread his hands. His smiling face, in the lamplight, was exhultant. "Who else? It was Joaquín! He blew his head off!"

"*Gracias a Dios,*" murmured Antonia.

Claudio slapped Luis on the back. *"Bueno! Esta muy bien!"* He hugged Luis in a wild dance.

When they stopped for breath, Luis told them, "We are all going home now. Joaquín wants you to meet him at Lake Tulare."

Claudio sobered. This was a last command, to get Antonia safely to Joaquín.

"So it is finished at last," he said. Then to Antonia, "We will leave in the morning."

"Not now?" Antonia was ready to go immediately. That's why she wore the trail clothes. All she had to do was slip on her boots.

"At daybreak," said Claudio. "Luis has been riding. Come, Luis, you will sleep on straw tonight."

"No, no," said Luis. "Since dawn I have been riding. First, I must satisfy a big thirst at the *cantina*." His face wrinkled in a broad, victorious grin. "No?"

"*Sí.* Yes, of course," said Claudio. "But I will sleep, so that one of us can take charge in the morning."

● ● ●

194

Before dawn's first light, Claudio had three horses saddled and provisioned to ride. As he led them to the front door of the adobe, the light in the bedroom went out. Antonia appeared in the doorway. She wore the long gown over her trail clothes, so as not to arouse suspicion. As she gathered the skirt to mount, she noticed Luis was not with them.

"Where is Luis?"

"He did not return last night."

"Oh, that stupid one—his big thirst."

Claudio grinned. "We'll stop at the *cantina*. I'm sure we'll find him there."

He guided his mount at a slow walk toward the center of town, leading Luis' saddled horse by the reins. Antonia followed.

As they entered the plaza, they saw a group of men gathered in front of the sheriff's office. Claudio guided the horses to the far side of the square.

"Something is wrong," he said.

In the darkness, all they could make out was the cluster of men in front of the one lighted building.

Antonia dismounted. "I'll find out," she said, and moved off into the darkness.

As she approached the group of men she saw they were the Rangers. Her heart beat faster, but she continued. As she passed the lighted sheriff's office, the men made way for her. A quick glance through the window revealed a drunk and disheveled Luis, sprawled in a chair, being questioned by the sheriff and Captain Love.

She walked on past the group of men and paused in a shadow between buildings.

It was only moments later that Love came out and addressed his Rangers.

"We'll be riding out before noon. Every man with full equipment."

"Where we headin', Captain?"

Captain Love lowered his voice, but Antonia heard him say, "This Murrieta has too many friends around here. If anyone should ask, tell them we're riding to Los Angeles."

In the first light of dawn, as Claudio unsaddled Luis' horse and turned it into a small corral behind the adobe, Antonia said, "We must reach them first to warn them, and to make other plans."

"I have been thinking," said Claudio. "They will not leave until noon. We can reach Joaquín and the others well ahead of these Rangers. It will give us time to plan where we will meet them, and kill them."

In the dawn light, Antonia looked closely at this favorite cousin of Joaquín's, who looked so much like her beloved husband that only the eyes and the freckles distinguished one from the other. In Claudio, she could see Joaquín and her heart overflowed with tenderness.

Now that Captain Roberts was dead, all thought of vengeance had left her mind. All she could think of now was to be reunited with the man she loved, to live in peace, and bear his sons in a happy home far from these terrible *Americanos*.

"Or we could flee," she said hopefully.

Claudio's eyes widened, surprised by her changed attitude.

"That will be for Joaquín to decide," he said.

He mounted lightly and turned his horse toward *el*

196

Camino Real, the coast highway, heading south. "Come! It will be a long, hard ride," he added, putting spurs to his mount.

It was well after sunset when Claudio and Antonia arrived at the camp on Lake Tulare.

After the greetings and embraces, after the news of the Ranger's close pursuit was told, while Joaquín still held Antonia in his arms, she said softly, "Let us end this and go home."

Surprised and pleased by her change of heart, he raised his head to look into her eyes. "You mean that?" he asked seriously. "It was for you that I swore a vow, remember?"

She pressed her head against his chest. *"Caro mio,* that vow is more than fulfilled. Now that Captain Roberts is dead, I want only to go home and live in peace with the man I love."

Joaquín's pulse beat faster at those words. For three years Antonia had been not wife, nor woman, but only a spirit of vengeance. For three years they had slept beside each other, but never together. He placed a hand under her chin and gently raised her face to his. "Do you mean that your vow also is now fulfilled, that you will once more be Rosita Felix, the girl that I married, my wife?"

Shyly, she pressed her face into the hollow of his throat. "For the rest of my life," she whispered. "That's all I want."

Passion, hunger, raced like a fire in his veins, as he kissed the top of her head and breathed the perfume of her midnight hair.

Over her head, he looked at the men clustered about

the campfire, talking about the pursuit of the California Rangers. He had already told them that there would be no more killing, that when Antonia and Claudio joined them they would all be going back to Sonora. There was no need to change that because of the Rangers. They could easily lose Love and his men in the maze of canyons and passes in the Sierra Nevada mountains.

But now there was need of change for another reason. He wanted to travel alone with this woman who was once again his wife. Love rekindled. Nights of passion under the stars. A wildfire coursed in his veins. Gently, he led Antonia to a seat by the fire.

"These two have had a hard ride," he told the men. "But we must leave this place. It is too open and unprotected."

"*Sí,*" agreed Claudio. "These Rangers are following us. They will be coming through the same pass through the mountains, by way of Priest Valley. We could ride back. Meet them in an ambush when they ride through, in the morning, and kill them all."

Joaquín put an arm about his beloved cousin. "No, no, my cousin, my friend!" He laughed lightly. "That is a good plan but, God willing, we will do no more killing. Not even these Rangers. We are all going home."

The others murmured, but not in disagreement.

"This is what I want you to do," Joaquín continued. "Ride back along the trail and sleep this night with guards posted. Then, first thing at dawn, wipe out the tracks leading toward this camp and then ride north in the San Joaquín valley, leaving a plain trail. These Rangers will follow your tracks and, when you see they are behind you, lead them into these Sierra Nevada mountains and lose them as you head back to Sonora."

He paused, waiting for any dissent. There was none, so he said, "In a few days we will all meet in Sonora and have a grand celebration."

"You mean you're not coming with us?" asked Claudio.

"No, my cousin," said Joaquín. "You can do this last thing without me. Antonia needs sleep. We will leave at the break of day and meet you in my father's house when you get to Sonora."

About this same time, westward, on *el Camino Real*, the Rangers were entering King City.

Love gave orders that the horses be fed grain and bedded in the livery stable. "We'll get a decent meal and sleep in soft beds tonight," he told the men.

That was welcome news and some of the Rangers headed for the brightly lighted Nugget Saloon, others for the restaurant.

It was about ten o'clock when they finished their meal. The proprietor, a florid-faced Dutchman from Pennsylvania, brought a big, blue agate coffeepot to the table where Love, Henderson, and two of the Rangers sat.

As he refilled their cups, he asked, "You on the trail of the bandit, Murrieta?"

"We are," said Love.

The proprietor nodded. He set the coffeepot on a nearby table where four other Rangers were eating and came back.

"I think they were here."

"When?"

"Late this afternoon."

"What makes you think it was Murrieta?"

The big Dutchman tugged at his mustache. "Well, he was a young, slim, good-lookin' greaser. He had this woman with him. She was a beauty. They'd been riding hard. They didn't say much. Just ate and left. But I've seen his picture on the poster. It was Murrieta."

Love was instantly attentive. The description fit. But their information was that Joaquín Murrieta was at Lake Tulare.

"When was this?" he asked.

"About four, four-thirty."

"What did they say? They must have said something."

"No. Like I told you, they didn't talk much."

"Did you hear anything?"

Again, pulling at his mustache, the proprietor frowned, trying to remember.

"They talked Spanish, you know, and I don't know Spanish."

"A word," Love prompted. "Anything you remember."

"Well, when they finished eating, he said, *'vamos.'* I know that means, let's go. Then there was one other word I recognized, 'Tulare.' Could he of meant Lake Tulare?"

"It could be." Love was smiling now. "What's the best way to Lake Tulare from here?"

"Priest Valley," said the proprietor. "There's a pass through the mountains about a mile south of here."

Love nodded. All signs of fatigue from the day's long ride had left him. The trail was hot. He glanced at

Henderson, then back to the proprietor. "Thank you very much," he said.

"My pleasure. I hope you get him. Any more coffee?"

"No. No, thank you. It was a fine supper."

The big Dutchman smiled and moved away. Love turned to his men. "We're getting close."

"I know that pass," said Henderson. "That's rough country. You ain't thinking—"

"Yes, I am. There's a moon tonight. We're gettin' close and a night ride will put us that much closer."

"That's dangerous country," insisted Henderson. "They call these mountains, *El Diablo*, the Devil. And the men are tired."

"So am I," said Love. "But you're going to lead us through that pass. And we're going to ride tonight."

He turned to one of the Rangers sitting with them. "George, go tell the men. They've got two hours to rest. They can sleep or not, but we assemble at the livery stable at midnight."

"Right, Captain." George Evans stood. He tilted his Army hat at a cocky, jaunty angle. "But they won't like it."

"Go on, tell 'em! And square that hat. This ain't no promenade we're going on."

Chapter 19

Joaquín awakened to instant awareness. And the first thing he was aware of was the warm body curled against his, one slim arm resting across his bare chest, under the blankets.

Stars blazed in the blackness of the night and he wondered what time it was. Then he heard a bird call and, as he listened, other twitterings and birdsong announced the hour before dawn. Far out in the lake, a fish splashed, breaking the surface.

The warmth of Antonia's body, the perfume of her hair, intoxicated him. The wildfire flashed in his veins and he kissed her awake, murmuring soft endearments. Antonia responded with an eager willingness, giggling like a young girl, as her hands caressed and gripped his body as if she would never let him go, never get enough of him.

With the roar of a young bull he ravished her, and the instant passion left them limp and breathless.

"My pigeon, my dove," he whispered, holding her head to his breast, "now you are Rosita Felix again, my woman, my wife."

"So long . . . it has been so long," she said regretfully.

"Too long. A whole lifetime, it seems, since I've kissed my wife," and he pressed his lips to hers gently, in a kiss of loving tenderness and compassion that far outweighed the tumult of their sex.

He was bursting with happiness, overflowing with a joy and vigor that seemed boundless, full of plans for their future. But the outlaw trail had given him instincts of survival he would never lose.

Dawn had already lighted the sky, birds flashed in the forest, a mist was rising over the lake. Their horses stirred and began grazing the grass where they were tethered.

Joaquín threw aside the blanket. He pulled on boots and shirt, and stood to buckle his guns.

"Get dressed," he said. "We'll start home without eating. After we've ridden several hours, and are high in the mountains, we will stop for food."

He moved away, toward the horses. When he brought them back, saddled, Antonia was dressed and had the blankets rolled.

She mounted her horse lightly. The expression on her face was as joyful as a young bride's as she reached out to touch Joaquín's hand as he tied her blanket roll to the back of her saddle.

He kissed her hand, then moved to tie his own blanket to his saddle. As he was fastening the straps, gunshots sounded faintly to the west.

It was full daylight.

Joaquín paused, looking back over the San Joaquín valley. As far as the eye could see, there was no sign of life or movement.

More gunshots sounded, faint and far away.

He mounted and looked westward from this higher

elevation, standing in the stirrups.

In the whole length and breadth of the valley, there was no sign of movement. Nothing.

The first shots were fired by Claudio at the riders who suddenly appeared, not thirty yards from where they had encamped in the darkness of the previous night.

Three-Fingered Jack and Claudio had taken the last watch. At daybreak, while Jack started a fire and prepared breakfast, Claudio watered the horses and had begun to saddle his own horse when the first of the strangers rode up, out of an arroyo, appearing as if out of nowhere.

The stranger, who was Captain Love in the lead of his file of Rangers, came riding toward the camp calling a cheery, "Good morning."

Instantly alert, Claudio called back, "Who are you?" And he reached for his gun.

"Hold it!" Love had him covered instantly.

By this time a second rider, Henderson, had emerged from the arroyo.

"Cover that man," ordered Love and Henderson drew and aimed his six-gun at Claudio.

Other riders were filing up out of the arroyo. The sleeping men of the band scrambled out of their blankets, reaching for boots and guns in startled confusion. Jack turned toward the strangers, the coffeepot in his right hand, and Love saw that he had only three fingers.

By this time the gambler, Burns, had come up with the others. Claudio recognized him instantly and realized these were the California Rangers. The pursuit had been closer than they thought.

Taken by surprise, Burns exclaimed, "That's them!" Then shouted a warning, "Joaquín! These are the Rangers!"

Claudio dropped his saddle, drew, and fired three quick shots at the riders and leaped on the bare back of his horse, jabbing with spurs and reaching for the trailing reins. Three-Fingered Jack drew his revolver, fired at Love, and threw the coffeepot at the strangers. The sleeping camp suddenly erupted in a blaze of gunfire as the rest of the Rangers came galloping up and exchanged shots with the members of the band.

In the confusion Claudio darted away, followed by Henderson and Lafayette Black. Jack, with no chance to reach the horses, scrambled into the chaparral on foot, with Love, George Evans, and John Nuttall after him.

In that first exchange of gunfire, the gambler, Burns, was killed. Whether by a bullet from the gang, or by a Ranger bullet, for having shouted that warning, will never be known.

What happened to the others is well known. Told over and over in newspaper accounts and magazine interviews, recalled by the men who lived through it until the day they died, and documented in official files as the report of the California Rangers to the legislature, in the court trial of the surviving members of the outlaw band, and in payment of the rewards for the "capture or death" of the bandits.

The night ride of the Rangers, which led to their surprise appearance in the outlaw camp, had been uneventful. By moonlight, Henderson guided them through the dangerous pass, walking the horses in single file, some of the riders dozing in the saddle when, at times, Henderson dismounted to test an especially risky section on foot. At dawn, they reached the end of the mountain area and looked out over the broad San Joaquín Valley.

The Rangers dismounted to stretch and relieve themselves.

A few miles away, in the vast expanse of the valley, a slim column of smoke from a campfire was rising in the still morning air.

"It must be a band of *vaqueros* rounding up cattle or wild horses," said Love, squinting into the distance against the rising sun.

Henderson nodded agreement. "It couldn't be Murrieta," he said. "Lake Tulare's a good thirty miles across that valley."

"Anyhow, we'll check 'em. Maybe get some information."

"And maybe a cup of hot coffee," added George Evans, who had come up to stand with them as they looked at the distant smoke.

Harry Love glanced around at him.

"Listen, something's been bothering me," he said. "Get the men over here."

When the men were gathered, Love looked at them. They all wore their Army hats, the only piece of uniform clothing Love had been able to acquire when he organized the Rangers. Now he realized why it had annoyed him when George Evans cocked his hat the night before in the restaurant.

"I want you to take those hats off," he told the men. "They're going to be able to see us a long way off when we cross this valley. Without the hats, they may think

206

we're cowboys, or some miners. If they don't know who we are, it'll give us an advantage."

There was disagreement. In the gold fields, a hat was almost as essential to survival as was a gun, but there was logic in the captain's reasoning. The men took off their hats.

"Mount up!" ordered Love. "We'll follow this dry creek bed. It's going toward that campfire and I want to see who's out there."

"That's the Cantua arroyo," said Henderson.

Love nodded. The name meant nothing to him but it was routine procedure to seek whatever concealment was available.

He mounted and led off with the men following in single file.

It was Saturday morning, the twenty-fourth of July, 1853.

In the chaparral, Three-Fingered Jack had a slight advantage in that he had some concealment while the Rangers, on horseback, stood out as plain targets against the morning sky.

Crawling through underbrush and across arroyos, dodging and darting through places the horsemen had to ride around, he emptied his gun at the pursuing men. For half a mile, he eluded them, stopping only to reload and fire. Two of the Rangers' horses were shot dead, but still they came on, pouring a random fire at any glimpse of the fleeing man.

Stopping behind a boulder to reload, Jack felt a scorching, tearing hammerblow on his exposed right shoulderblade. He dove into a shallow arroyo and crawled along it, feeling the strength drain from his body. When he could go on no more, he fell back against the side of the arroyo. He could hear the calls and hoofbeats of the pursuing Rangers closing in. His vision was blurring. His strength was gone. He knew he was dying.

As the sounds of pursuit came closer, he raised his gun, supporting it with both hands. Shadows came into his dimming sight. He pointed the heavy weapon at them as he heard a loud voice.

It was Love calling for him to surrender.

With his last strength, Jack squeezed his final bullet at the sound of that voice and Love shot him between the eyes.

By this time, Claudio, riding like an Indian, clinging low on his horse with legs and one arm while he fired back at Henderson and Black, was a mile or more from the camp.

The two Rangers were gaining on him, but he wheeled his horse suddenly and, holding to the far side of the animal, shot over the horse's back at his pursuers. He hit Black's horse with his sixth bullet and saw the Ranger thrown to the ground.

He swung his body up, drew his other six-gun, and wheeled his horse in a different direction. Now Henderson was his only pursuer, riding a good thirty yards behind. Claudio changed direction one more time, shooting by feel from the bounding animal. The change gave Henderson a broader target and one of the Ranger's bullets struck the horse. It stumbled and Claudio hit the ground, tumbling, holding to his gun.

Shaken, he arose on one knee for a last stand. Henderson drew his mount to a rearing stop. The two men fired at the same instant. Claudio missed. Henderson did not. And the Ranger sat there on his trembling, heaving horse and fired three more bullets through the young outlaw's body.

Claudio Carillo was twenty-three years old when he died in 1853.

At the camp, the Rangers had killed or captured the other members of the outlaw band.

In all, Claudio, Three-Fingered Jack, and four others of the band were dead. Florencio Crúz and José Ochovo were captured alive. Several of the Rangers were wounded, five of their horses had been shot dead as well as the gambler, Burns.

It was a gruesome sight, but their job was done and the Rangers were hungry after their all-night ride.

While the wounded were being treated, two of the Rangers started to prepare breakfast, using the same campfire and the same pot of beans Three-Fingered Jack had been preparing for the outlaw gang. One of them recovered the battered coffeepot, refilled it, and pushed it into the hot embers.

As they ate, with the bodies of dead men and dead horses strewn about them, their conversation centered on the split of the reward money. Elated with their victory, they made extravagant claims of bravado and plans for spending the money.

"They jest might not be no reward money," one sober voice silenced the high spirits of the others.

The Rangers stopped talking for a moment, then laughed and hooted at the absurdity of that supposition.

"All right, what proof have we got?" asked the lone

Ranger. "I don't even know if that is Murrieta we killed. Do you?"

"Burns said it was him, didn't he?" argued one of the men.

"Sure, he even called him, 'Joaquín,' " said another.

"But Burns ain't here no more. Now what are we gonna do, ride back to San Francisco and jest tell the governor that we killed Murrieta and that ole Three-Fingers? You think he's gonna pay out the reward on our say-so?"

That gave the Rangers something to think about. Silently, they went on chewing their food, lost in thought.

After a while, Love said, "He's right." He finished the last of his coffee and stood up. "We've got to take back some valid proof."

He paced over to the body of Murrieta and stood looking down at it for a long moment. Then he went to one of the saddled horses and got a half-empty bag of salt and a hand axe.

"Lafayette, get over here and bring that log you're sitting on."

At the body, Love turned and faced the men.

"We got a four or five day ride ahead, right?"

The men nodded agreement.

"And if we carry these bodies back, they're gonna start to stink in two days, right?"

The men nodded again. Lafayette Black moved up beside his captain, holding the piece of wood, and wondering what for.

Love reached down and grasped the hair of Murrieta's head and lifted the head slightly.

"Put that wood under his neck," he said.

Black slid the log in and Love handed him the axe.

"Now chop it off."

Black hesitated momentarily, then swung the axe.

Love lifted the dripping head by its hair. He held it a moment, looking at the staring eyes, the half-open mouth, then dropped it into the sack of salt.

One of the Rangers vomited up his breakfast. Others gagged and murmured and turned away.

"That proof enough?" said Harry Love.

The ones who could still look at him agreed.

"Come on, Lafayette." Love moved to the body of Three-Fingered Jack.

Jack's head was so mutilated by the bullet that had finished him, Love chose another means of identification.

"Chop off his hand," he ordered.

Lafayette Black chopped it off at the wrist. Love put the three-fingered hand in the sack and tied the sack to the back of his saddle. Valid proof for the Governor. He then ordered the Rangers to break camp. Their job was done. They were going home.

By the lake shore, Joaquín and Antonia sat their horses, looking back over the vast range of the San Joaquín Valley.

It was broad daylight. In the distance, the valley shimmered in the sun's rays, but there was no sign of life or movement. There had been several more bursts of gunfire, then complete silence.

Joaquín looked around at Antonia. He saw the apprehension in her eyes.

"Whatever it was," he said, "we can do nothing now."

Joaquín turned his horse.

"*Vamos,*" he said softly. When there was no response from Antonia, he reached over to turn her mount by its halter.

Then he spurred his horse and they galloped along the lake shore into the rising sun, heading for the High Sierras.

Chapter 20

Leaving the bodies of the bandits, of the gambler, Burns, and all the dead horses for the coyotes and vultures, the Rangers started back to San Francisco with their two captured prisoners. To end the first day's ride, they stopped at the nearest Army post at what is now Fresno.

There they turned over the prisoners, to be held for a U.S. marshal, and the post doctor preserved the head and hand in bottles of alcohol. He told Love, "The priest at Merced knew him well. He could give you a positive identification."

The following day the Rangers rode into the plaza at Merced. The bottles, slung one on each side of a pack horse, caused an instant commotion.

The square filled with men and women and children, all Mexican, or *Chileno*, all jabbering in excited Spanish, all pushing to get a look at the bottles and their gruesome contents.

Love gave the order to dismount. The riders swung down and tied their horses to hitching racks. They gathered about their captain for further orders, with the men and children of Merced surrounding them, asking questions, pointing and arguing back and forth among themselves.

"We'll get a meal here, then move out of town to camp for the night," Love told his men. Then he addressed the crowd: "Would one of you ask the priest to come here?"

One of the men pushed forward. He spoke good English.

"*Sí*. My son will bring the good father." He pushed a youth toward the church, speaking a few words in Spanish, then turned back, smiling up at Captain Love.

"What is this thing in the bottle?" he asked.

"Don't you know? Don't you recognize him?"

The man spread his hands. "Should I?"

"You know the bandit, Murriéta, don't you?"

"Bandit? No. We know Joaquín. He is no bandit to us."

"Well, is that Joaquín?" Love asked.

The man spoke in rapid Spanish to several of the crowd. They all peered at the head, floating in alcohol, the hair waving like seaweed with each movement of the bottle. They discussed it in Spanish, gesturing and pointing and arguing heatedly.

Finally, the man who had spoken first turned back to Love. He wrinkled his brow and pushed his lower lip up, shaking his head negatively. "No. This is not Joaquín."

An old hag of a woman pulled at Love's sleeve.

"*Sí*, it is him!" She nodded vigorously. "Joaquín," she said positively. "The one they call Murriéta!"

That started an explosion of conflicting Spanish,

some of the crowd shouting down the old woman, some of them confirming her statement.

A young woman shoved the old hag aside. She struck an arrogant pose in front of Harry Love, hands on hips, a sneer on her full, carmined lips.

"You think this is Murrieta?" She snorted with lusty, peasant contempt. "Ha! I tell you, you will never kill Joaquín Murrieta! He is like the wind"—she made a sudden sweeping gesture—"an avenging angel—"

A cheer from the crowd covered the rest of her words. Love glanced at his Rangers for support and they moved closer about him. The cheers died suddenly.

The priest, in long black gown, and the boy were coming from the church. The now silent crowd parted. The priest walked up to Captain Love, smiling, his hand extended.

"Welcome. Be at home here." It was Father Cordova. He shook hands with Love and greeted the other Rangers. "Can I be of some service?"

"Yes, *Padre*," said Love. "I was told you know Murrieta."

"*Sí*. I am his confessor and his friend."

"Well, would you tell me"—Love pointed—"is that his head in the bottle?"

Father Cordova looked in the direction Love pointed. The grisly sight shocked him. He shuddered. He closed his eyes and crossed himself. Then raised the crucifix which hung at his breast against the evil omen, and spoke in Latin. The crowd edged away from the bottle and gathered behind their priest.

"Look at it, *Padre*! And tell me if that is the head of Murrieta!"

Father Cordova opened his eyes. He looked about at the Rangers, at the crowd of his parishioners, as if he had come back from another world. Then he moved slowly toward the pack horse to which the two bottles were strapped. The swarm of parishioners moved with him. He stopped. They stopped. He stood at a distance, frowning severely at the bottle and its horrid contents.

His mind was racing. At first sight, from a distance, he'd thought it was Joaquín. Closer, he saw the barely perceptible freckles, the green of the staring eyes, and knew that it was Claudio. Also knew that to end this pursuit and bloodshed, he would have to tell a lie. As a man of God, a servant of Jesus Christ, the son of God, who said, "thou shalt not bear false witness," he must speak this lie.

He spoke softly in Spanish to some of the men close by, telling them to agree with whatever he said. "Tell the others," he whispered in Spanish. Then turned back to the Rangers.

"Well, is it him?" asked Love.

Father Cordova stepped closer, fingering the cross at his breast.

"Is that the head of Murrieta?" demanded Love.

Father Cordova stopped when he was face to face with Harry Love. He raised his eyes to the *Americano's*. He gripped his cross, praying silently that God would forgive him, and spoke a false witness.

"*Sí*, that is Murrieta."

Behind him, surrounding them, the townspeople broke into loud cheers, substantiating the priest's identification.

Love drew a deep breath. He'd been worried, uncertain of his victory after all they had been through. He

216

said, "Would you write a statement to that effect, *Padre*?"

Father Cordova nodded. "Come with me."

As the priest and Captain Love walked toward the church, the townspeople of Merced began to congratulate the Rangers. Boisteriously praising these *gringos*, and all the townspeople identified the head of Murrieta. Who should know better than they? Hadn't they received gold and guns and horses from him? *Gringo* gold. *Gringo* guns and horses. And hadn't they known Murrieta, the Avenger, face to face? Hadn't they sat with him to share a drink, and play three-card monte?

And now that Murrieta was dead, they cheered the *gringo*.

It was a good act.

The Rangers made one more stop before reaching San Francisco. In San Bruno, they received another sworn statement from the former Alcalde of that city. It was the statement of authenticity later printed on advertising posters when the bottles were displayed in saloons and other public places, the head and the three-fingered hand always being exhibited at the same time and together.

It read:

State of California—County of San Francisco, ss: Ignacio Lisarraga, of Sonora, being duly sworn, says: That he has seen the alleged head of Joaquín, now in the possession of Captain Love's Rangers. That deponent was well acquainted with Joaquín Murrieta, and that the head is and was the veritable head of Joaquín Murrieta, the celebrated Bandit. And further says not.

Sworn to before me, this 28th day of July, A.D., 1853

Chas. D. Carter, Notary Public

Clear and blazing sunlight lay over all the peaceful valley of the *hacienda* Carillo, in Sonora. A blue and cloudless sky arched incredibly high and wide.

From where he sat his horse on a high place overlooking the valley, Joaquín looked down a two-mile slope of knee-high grassland, where bands of the golden Palomino horses roamed free, to the buildings and corrals grouped about his father's house.

He had galloped ahead to get the first sight of his homeland. As Antonia came up beside him, he dismounted and reached up to swing her down beside him. Together, holding her in his arms, they viewed the peaceful valley, all green and gold in the hot sun of Mexico.

"At last," he said, and crushed her to his bosom in a fierce hug and kiss.

Antonia squealed with delight. Again the child-bride, she clung to him for dear life, kissing his face and throat and gasping words of love.

He released her and they stood a moment, breathless with a joy indescribable, as they looked at each detail of this familiar scene. Then Joaquín suddenly knelt beside her and began digging at the earth with his Bowie knife.

"What—?" Antonia began, taken by surprise.

"One last thing," he grunted, as he dug deeper, and

scooped out earth, until he had a hole big enough to bury a small dog.

Then he stood, grinning at her.

"*Caro mio!* What is this!" Antonia wanted to know.

Still grinning, Joaquín unbuckled his gunbelt and held it high before him. The grin faded. For a long moment, he looked at the heavy weapons with evident revulsion, then dropped them into the hole.

He pushed earth over them with his foot, and stamped it down, until the hole was filled.

"That is the end!" he said. "Murrieta is no more."

He caught Antonia's hand in his.

"Henceforth, I am Joaquín Carillo and you are no more, Antonia." He looked at her with such loving tenderness that it brought an ache to Antonia's throat. "You are again Rosita Felix Carillo, my wife."

Eyes brimming with tears, she looked up at this man, the only man she had ever loved since she was a little girl. She nodded, silently, because the lump in her throat was choking her.

There was nothing more to say. It was over. They mounted their horses and rode slowly toward the buildings in the valley. Then faster and faster, side by side, the horses carrying them as they had ridden together in the many raids upon the *Americanos*.

Distantly, across the vast sunlit valley, it seemed, a faint cry echoed:

"*Yo soy Joaquín!*"

The scattered bands of golden horses, grazing on the slope, heard something. They looked up at the riders bearing down upon them. They began to stir, to move, then run in a stampede which surrounded and engulfed the two galloping riders.

From the hilltop, in all that wide, peaceful valley with its blue sky arching to infinity, Joaquín and Rosita were but bobbing specks in the center of the herd of thundering horses, running free, running home.

Again, above the thunder of hooves, that distant cry echoed out of nowhere:

"Yo soy Joaquín!"